GOOD GIRL BAD

S.A. MCEWEN

Published by Kaleido Text Media

First published in Australia 2022

ISBN: 9780645211009 (ebook)

ISBN: 9780645211023 (paperback)

Editor: Erica Russikoff, Erica Edits

Cover Design: Rough—Draft @rghdrftstudio

Disclaimer

For Mum,

Who keeps on keeping on, and gives so much, even when we're troublesome.

Thank you for everything.

1

The house is silent.

Eerily so.

Rebecca Giovanni stands at the top of the small stairway to the kitchen. Below her, her sixteen-year-old daughter Tabitha's miniature poodle, Charlie, lies on his side. He could nearly be sleeping, except he never sleeps in the kitchen, on the cold tiles. Rebecca can see that something is wrong, the position of his legs not quite right, his little head stretched back at an unusual angle, a rigidity about him sufficient information such that Rebecca does not go any closer; does not check.

Beyond him, the front door is wide open. A cold wind blows in from the street, through the leaves of the wisteria hanging lushly around the veranda, caressing Rebecca's forearms, swirling beyond her into the silent house.

The faint scent—her favorite flower—drifts past her toward the very back of the house, where her youngest daughter Genevieve is still sleeping. At fourteen, she is well and truly a teen when it comes to sleeping in. The house could fall apart around her and she would not so much as mumble a complaint. Rather, she'd roll over, tugging the doona around her ears, eyes resolutely shut against the intrusion.

It's spring—November—but still cold, and Rebecca shivers.

Leroy was not in their bed, and Tabitha was not in hers, either.

Rebecca's eyes roam around the kitchen.

She is not worried yet.

She notices Leroy's phone and wallet next to the fruit bowl; he has not gone far.

Tabby's phone, usually glued to her hand, is hanging precariously over the edge of the dining table. It looks like it should be falling, not balancing there.

But other than that, the house looks much the same as it always does when Rebecca gets up.

Rebecca is still not worried, despite the open front door, and despite the dead dog in her kitchen.

She's not worried yet.

But she will be.

2

Six Months Earlier

Rebecca smooths her Armani skirt across her thighs, a tiny, self-contained movement that she uses as a break in conversation. It makes her look calm and certain; it soothes her when she needs to take a moment to think of what it is she wants to say.

It also reminds her of who she is: successful. Capable. In charge. The mother who wears Armani to parent-teacher interviews, her makeup flawless, all poise and perfection.

Rebecca doesn't speak rashly. She weighs her words, her cool blue eyes resting on the recipient appraisingly. In this case, the recipient is Tabitha's home room teacher, Ms. Paisley.

"I'm not sure what you're getting at?" she says eventually, her gaze unflinching.

Ms. Paisley is young. Much younger than Rebecca, with kind brown eyes, which are right now blinking too frequently.

Nerves? Rebecca wonders.

She is used to people being nervous around her. Being wowed by her, in fact.

"Well, it's my first year teaching Tabby, of course," Ms.

Paisley responds, her words tumbling over each other in her haste to get them out. *It's probably your first year teaching, period,* Rebecca thinks to herself, patronizing, but she keeps herself in check. "So I've only known her for a few months, obviously. It's just, she's always been one of our top students, and certainly her work earlier in the year was of a consistently high quality. It's just the last month or so that things have started to slip a little. Work not handed in, or not much effort applied, that kind of thing." She nearly looks apologetic, but seems to be trying her best not to. Even as Rebecca watches, she pulls her shoulders back and sits up a little higher in her chair.

"I'll have a word with her. But she's been her usual self at home. I haven't noticed any changes." Here Rebecca stops. *Typical,* she thinks. Just as she was taking ownership—"I" haven't noticed any changes—she spots Nate fighting his way around chairs and parents to reach them. Rebecca watches him silently. It's characteristic of her ex-husband to be late, and to look the opposite of calm and poised. Rebecca wonders if people think less of her because she was once married to him; if she's tainted by association.

"Sorry I'm late," he puffs as he comes to a halt beside them, casting about for a spare chair he can pull up. Spying one halfway across the room, he disappears again. Rebecca turns back to Ms. Paisley, who looks as though she's very happy to wait for Nate to return.

Does no one have a sense of time and urgency except me? Rebecca thinks. If the roles were reversed, she would plough ahead without the late ex-husband. She would say what needed to be said to whomever was present, and conclude the meeting decisively, precisely on time. Too bad, so sad if you were late and missed half of it.

She runs her hand over her skirt again, the soft black fabric feeling expensive and luxurious under her touch. It clings to her thighs elegantly, ever so slightly suggestively, the muscle underneath nicely defined by regular weight classes and running. She raises her eyes to Nate again, her expression patient to anyone who didn't know her well.

To Nate, the patience is feigned, or mocking.

Here we are, waiting for you, again.

He seems unfazed though. He plonks the chair down next to Rebecca, and beams at Ms. Paisley.

"How's my girl doing?" he says, and Rebecca has to stop herself from rolling her eyes.

"We're well past that, Nate," she says, cutting Ms. Paisley off, and summarizing the meeting so far, her demeanor crisp and business-like. She doesn't give Nate a chance to respond, but addresses Ms. Paisley again with the air of someone who is used to making all the decisions.

"So, I'll have a word with her. I'm sure it's nothing to worry about. Tabby has always been a hard worker. If necessary, I can always limit her phone time. That's always rather motivating for her."

Ms. Paisley looks surprised, and starts to open her mouth, but Rebecca cuts her off. "Did you have any questions, Nate?"

"Yes, actually," he says, though he knows full well that the question was rhetorical, designed to show Ms. Paisley that they were co-parenting cooperatively. Rebecca didn't really expect him to say yes—to the point that she was half rising from her chair, and stops mid-air.

She glances at Nate, something hard passing across her face fleetingly, then she smiles and sits back down. Poised and gracious.

"Well, obviously we'll talk to her," Nate goes on, glancing at Rebecca. "But have you noticed anything at school that might explain it? Any change in her friendship group? Any boys she's hanging out with, that might be breaking her heart?" Nate looks like he is joking, making light of it, but Rebecca can see that he's just not sure how appropriate it is to ask Tabby's home room teacher about her love life, so he's disguising it under a protective, jovial father spiel.

Joke, joke, joke.

Rebecca thinks Nate is wasting his time. *Her* time.

Of course Tabby isn't seeing anyone.

Rebecca actively discourages relationships—she thinks Tabby is far too young, and has more important things to do. Like excel at school and get into a good university. The truth is, though, that Rebecca would have no idea if Tabby was romantically involved with anyone; they don't have that kind of relationship. Her certainty is rooted entirely in confidence that Tabby would not defy her wishes. She's not worried by Ms. Paisley's revelations. Tabby is strong-willed, and can be a little bit feisty, but she falls back into line when Rebecca flexes her parental rights.

For the briefest of moments, that reality is held up for her to examine, and the starkness of it feels uncomfortable, and nags at her. *Should she know her daughter better? Should her certainty be rooted in dialogue, not authority?* But she turns her thoughts back to the issue at hand.

"I very much doubt Tabby's been distracted by a boy," she says, somewhat pompously, and Ms. Paisley looks apologetic again.

"Well, actually, there has been a lot more socializing between the boys and girls this year, and I have noticed Tabby spending a lot of time with a particular young man, Trent Witherall. Has she mentioned him to you at all?"

Rebecca's demeanor shifts slightly, her posture stiffening, her jaw tensing. Nate glances at her uneasily.

"No, nothing," Rebecca says, her voice tight. She looks to Nate for confirmation, this time appearing genuinely interested in his response.

"She has mentioned Trent to me, yes," he says, directing his words to Ms. Paisley. "But she's never made it sound like they're dating, or that she likes him in particular. His name has just come up a few times when she's talking about her friends, what they're doing on the weekend. Do you think they're... seeing each other?" Nate is aware of something simmering in Rebecca next to him, and he keeps his eyes carefully on Ms. Paisley.

She, likewise, speaks back directly to Nate. "I would have thought so, yes," she says, but won't be drawn into why she thinks that. "I really think that's a conversation for you to have with your daughter, don't you think?" she hedges, and Nate wonders what she has seen.

Hand-holding?

Kissing?

Do kids kiss on school grounds these days? He can't even remember how you wooed girls back in his day. He can't imagine his broody eldest daughter being buffeted about by the strong feelings of young love.

But broodiness would be the perfect breeding ground for that intensity, that all-or-nothing consuming infatuation, wouldn't it?

Nate suddenly feels old and out of touch. Unlike Rebecca, he *has* noticed a change in his daughter. He would have said it had been much longer than this year though, and doubts very much it has anything to do with Trent Witherall. In fact, if his life depended on putting a date to it, he would have said it was a year or two ago that she started to become more withdrawn, more secretive. More broody.

About the time that Rebecca married that twerp, Leroy, in fact.

He steals a glance at his ex-wife. She is sitting very still, projecting that calm, reasonable, I-am-listening-to-you-deeply facade. He wonders if Ms. Paisley can see through it.

He wonders what sort of man *can't* see through it.

What sort of man would fall for it.

He did, sure. But he was so young.

You can't put an old head on young shoulders, his father used to tell him, and he understands the saying differently now.

But Leroy is his age. Forty-five, give or take a few years.

What was Leroy's excuse?

Or was he just as stupid as twenty-year-old Nate?

And if Leroy was just as stupid as a twenty-year-old, what might have gone on between him and Nate's sweet sixteen-year-old daughter, that might explain the changes in her mood?

BACK AT HOME, Rebecca dumps her handbag on the kitchen island with a loud thump.

She can hear chatter coming from the living room, the faint hum of the television, and she feels like storming up there and shutting it down, all of it. The television, the happy family time. Tabby has made her look stupid in front of her teacher, in front of Nate, but she's just glibly fooling around on a school night in front of the television without a care in the world.

"Tabby!" she shouts down the hallway, and there's a moment's silence, the voices quieting. Then the living room door opens and Leroy and Tabby both emerge, padding down the long hallway toward her. They look so easy, so relaxed, and she feels resentful that she has to be the one to bring things back to order, to interrupt their fun, to remind them of the real world.

But somebody has to do it.

But just as she opens her mouth to say something cross, something biting, Leroy jumps clownishly down the five steps into the kitchen and grabs her in a dance pose, swinging her around, one arm firmly around her waist. He grins at her impishly.

"Look out, Tabby, Becci looks a bit peeved! What is it? An F? An expulsion? You've learned that Tabby's quit math to do embroidery instead, and your dream of retiring on the back of your daughter's orthodontic practice has gone up in flames?"

He spins her around once more and then pushes her against the wall, kissing her right on the lips in front of Tabby, his eyes laughing.

They'll have sex tonight, she can tell from his kiss, the way he holds her against the wall.

Her tummy flutters.

"Slipping grades," she squeaks, as she tries to wriggle out of his grasp, but the tension has gone out of her.

Leroy gives her a final smooch, then releases her. As he turns to go back to the living room, to give her space to chat with Tabby, no doubt, she thinks she catches a small smile toward her daughter, and a wink, and her stomach does less of a flutter and more of a churn.

3

MONDAY

Rebecca shakes Genevieve roughly.

"Gen. Gen!" Genevieve groans, and tries to burrow back under her doona, but Rebecca is tugging it down harder and faster than she can pull it back up.

"Mom!" Gen protests, the cold creeping in from the hallway, from outside. From the situation in the kitchen.

"Where's your sister?" Rebecca's voice is urgent.

"Wha-at?" Genevieve rubs her bleary eyes. "How should I know?"

It's now nearly 9 a.m. Two hours have passed since Rebecca found the front door open, and impatience and irritation have finally given way to something more urgent.

"Get up," Rebecca instructs her youngest daughter, rifling in her cupboard and throwing a tee shirt and some leggings at her. Genevieve holds them up in confusion. They're not appropriate for a Melbourne spring morning, no matter that it's nearly summer. And they're certainly not appropriate for a school day.

"They're gone," Rebecca continues, looking through

Genevieve's wardrobe like she might find some clue in there. "Leroy. Tabby. Leroy's car. But something's not right. I can feel it."

Hustling Genevieve through the house, shivering in the thin tee shirt Rebecca had handed her, she points to the mobile phones and wallets triumphantly. "See? Tabby would never go anywhere without her phone. And. Charlie." Here she glances at the little form underneath the sweater she had hastily thrown over him while she made phone calls, trying to find her daughter and husband.

Her eyes linger there, uneasily.

In her state of agitation, she completely forgets how one ought to break such news to anyone, especially to her teenage daughter.

Genevieve is still half asleep, and is struggling to make sense of her mother's words, which are being thrown at her, staccato-like. Bam. Bam. Bam. Bam. But when her eyes—following Rebecca's—fall on the shape under the sweater, she falls silently to her knees. She glances up at Rebecca, a question in her eyes, but she doesn't need a response, and her mouth gapes slightly, tears welling in her eyes, and she doubles over, a silent scream emanating from her open mouth.

She doesn't touch the sweater, just keens silently beside the little body on the floor.

Something about her daughter's grief shakes Rebecca out of her quest for an explanation. Genevieve is a thoughtful, sensitive, quiet teen, and Rebecca is surprised by the force of her pain.

No, that's not right. She's not surprised by the force of it—she's surprised that Genevieve is showing it. To her mother.

Rebecca has her own pain about the dog, but it's been swallowed up by more important things, like where her husband and other daughter are, and why they left in such a hurry that they didn't even shut the front door.

She kneels beside Gen, putting her arms around her shuddering, small frame. "I'm sorry, I'm sorry," she whispers, mortified by her insensitivity. She holds Gen tight, keeping her close until her shaking slows and stills.

"What happened to him?" Gen hiccups, her voice painfully small.

"I don't know, sweetheart. But something's wrong. I'm going to call the police. I've already called everyone who I can think of who might know where they are."

She'd been methodical—Tabby's friends. Trent Witherall's parents. Nate. The school.

Miss Ambrosia, the cafe where Tabby works on Saturdays —only to be told that Tabby hadn't worked there for over four months.

Where was Tabby going on Saturdays, then?

Where was she getting money from?

Rebecca mentally kicks herself. She'd looked into GPS tracking when she'd bought Tabitha her first smartphone. For a while, she'd obsessively checked her location, but Tabby was always exactly where she said she'd be. Even after that interview with Ms. Paisley, when Rebecca was watching her closely, checking her location again daily—well, she'd gotten slack. She thought Ms. Paisley had it wrong. Tabby was never over in Richmond, where Trent lived. She was always with her best friend Freddy, studying, or else at work.

Rebecca had stopped checking. She really didn't think Tabby was the type to sneak around.

Now, though, she wonders what data she'd be able to access. Tabby's phone was right here. Didn't Google Maps keep data on everywhere you'd been? Was that true? And if it was, please dear God let Tabby's passcode be the same as it always was—the day she got Charlie, her twelfth birthday present. But he had arrived a week early, so it wasn't like she was using her *actual* birthdate, which Rebecca had told her a hundred times would be foolish, anyone could guess it.

Now, she grabs the phone off the table, presses the home button. Nothing. The phone is dead, and she scours around for a charger, usually lurking in every second power point, so many phones seemed to populate their home.

Personal phones. Work phones. Kids' phones.

Old, discarded phones.

Finally, she spies a cord hanging out from under the microwave, and plugs Tabby's phone in. It takes forever even for the little red battery symbol to blink on. Impatiently, she turns away from it.

"Did you know Tabby had quit Miss Ambrosia?" she asks Genevieve, trying to be gentle, but it's hard to keep the urgency, the accusing tone out of her voice.

The girl has pulled Charlie's stiff little body onto her lap. So different from Tabby, Genevieve is short and dark-haired, her brown eyes now staring vacantly into the distance. Charlie was Tabby's dog, but Tabby shared him generously with her little sister. She made sure to give Genevieve turns walking and feeding him, so the dog loved them both eagerly, joyously. Right above her, in fact, is an enlarged photo of the three of them. Charlie is clutched between the two girls, the love on their faces palpable through the camera lens. Tabby is crouched down—she's easily a foot taller than Gen. Her long, blonde hair is sun-bleached and messy, cascading over a slim, tan shoulder. Her blue eyes sparkle, staring right at you out from the wall.

Rebecca shivers. Leroy loves that picture. "Bottled joy" he called it, insisting that it was the one they frame, but it's always made Rebecca uneasy. Tabby looks older than she ought to in it. In a tank top and tiny shorts, she looks worldly, seductive. When she'd snapped at Leroy that perhaps that was why he liked it, he'd looked at her strangely. She still can't quite fathom the look that he gave her.

"They look like happy kids," he'd said, and she wondered if he could sense her jealousy, if that was why he was so restrained. God, she was basically accusing him of lusting after her teenage daughter, he was well within his rights to fly completely off the handle. Instead, that strange look. Like he didn't even know who she was in that moment.

It wasn't as simple as the ageing mother envying the blossoming of youthful beauty. Rebecca herself was beautiful, she had no doubt and no insecurity about that. Tabby even looked a lot like her, really. Taller and slimmer, but their features were similar, their striking blue eyes.

No, it wasn't that. But it was hard to put her finger on the pang that the picture gave her, every time.

She wished she'd put her foot down, ordered a different print.

Now, though, she focuses back on Genevieve, who solemnly shakes her head.

Rebecca has no reason to doubt her. Gen has always been compliant, cautious, responsible. Tabby is more like her, Rebecca—impulsive, flamboyant. Sure of herself.

Or at least, she used to be.

Is she still flamboyant?

Things have changed, Rebecca knows that. But they've changed so slowly, so incrementally, that she hasn't paid that much attention. Now, though, she realizes that the word *flamboyant* no longer applies to her eldest daughter.

Genevieve, on the other hand, was never flamboyant. Genevieve is steady. Calm. Rebecca trusts her absolutely.

Rebecca casts her mind back to the Saturday just gone. Tabby had left on her bike at about 11 a.m. as she always did. She covered the lunch shift, making coffees and toasting fancy baguettes for a little café one suburb over from them. Or at least, that was what she was supposed to be doing. Rebecca was sure, in fact, that Tabby had boasted of a promotion not that long ago. Managing that shift. Definitely not more than four months ago.

So where had she been going every Saturday for four hours?

"Did you call Freddy?" Gen's voice is faint. Rebecca thinks that she hasn't grasped the seriousness of the situation. All she can think about is the damn dog. And the dog definitely needs thinking about, but right now, Rebecca just wants to know where Leroy and Tabitha are.

"Yes. I spoke to Fred. They haven't seen her this weekend. Freddy had already left for school by the time I called."

Fred and Frederica. For the hundredth time, Rebecca thinks *how vain. Silly*, even. To choose a name for your kid that's basically the same as your own. The amount of times there's been confusion over who is being referred to when you say "Freddy" is ridiculous.

Tabby and Freddy have been best friends since grade four, and Fred, the father, has promised he'll get Freddy to call Rebecca when she gets home from school, in case she knows anything. The way he says it makes Rebecca's stomach churn again.

In case she knows anything.

But Rebecca shoves that feeling aside and calls the police.

4

By the time Nate arrives, the police have already been at Rebecca's house for an hour.

A bored-looking officer stops him at the door, asking for identification and a reason for being there.

"My daughter is bloody missing with *that man!*" He has to stop himself from shouting the last two words, his voice rising unusually high.

Rebecca looks over at him, disdain written all across her face. Even disdainful, she's still a striking woman, with her aquiline nose and astonishing blue eyes. She's fitter than when they were together, too—always shapely, she's now toned as well, and her posture is that of a lioness, queen of her terrain.

The officer's ears prick up at Nate's tone, though. "We don't have any reason to suspect anything suspicious at this stage, sir," he says. "But can you tell me why you refer to Mr. Giovanni in that manner?"

Nate can't though. He's never gotten along with Leroy, but do you usually get along with your replacement in the husband department? Leroy is too smooth, too handsome, and Nate is sure he'd be a player. The thought of him living with his teenage daughters is a constant thorn in his side. When Leroy had first moved in, he'd had to be very firm with Rebecca about some boundaries.

Leroy can't shower the girls.

He can't be in the bathroom with them.

At the time, they'd been ten and twelve, and Rebecca had just nodded and smiled sarcastically at him, but he could see how close she was to rolling her eyes. Because of course the girls didn't need any help in the shower, and of course even Rebecca would have thought it weird if her new boyfriend had wanted to spend time in the bathroom with her tween daughters. Rebecca was clearly humoring him. But she didn't know men the way that he, Nate, knew men. Tabitha was a knockout. Even at twelve, men did double takes on the street. She looked like she was a model, with those long, lean, tanned legs and waist-length beach-blonde hair. She didn't look away, either. She'd fix those smoldering eyes on whoever stared, her face deadpan, neither shy nor embarrassed nor egotistical.

He often wondered what went on behind her eyes, but he never asked.

She was going to break hearts, though, and Nate would be damned if he'd let a grown man spend any time with her naked.

Now, though, he's forced to backtrack. Because what could he say?

The man would have to be blind to not ogle her, to not notice her in a sexual manner?

No. He was being ridiculous. He knew that. He was just paranoid. You hear so many awful things these days. It was a terrible time to have a daughter.

To be a woman, he corrects himself. *It was a terrible time to be a woman. Or had it always been a terrible time, and now they were just starting to shout about it?* #MeToo had shaken him. And then there was the "incident" on Messenger. Here he cringes slightly, the police officer watching him curiously. It was all too difficult to think about, and he's whittled it down to a simple concept, one which was, however, impossible to enforce: *he did not want men thinking about his daughter in a sexual manner at all.*

Ever.

For the rest of her life.

Did all fathers feel like this? It was a constant mild panic, a sense of tension he could never quite shake. How dangerous the world might be for someone so beautiful.

Now, he wishes he'd asked what Tabby was thinking behind that blank expression when men stared at her. At the time, it was too uncomfortable. Embarrassing, even. What do you say to your daughter about men his age staring at her on the street? He always felt mortified, as though he was part of that group, like he needed to collectively apologize, like he was tainted by their stares, too. Like she might think less of him because weren't they all just a little bit like him? On the surface, at any rate. He couldn't quite put his finger on it. But it was awful and uncomfortable and he pretended it wasn't happening at all.

Now, he wishes he had some idea what her views were on middle-aged men. He wishes he'd been more proactive in talking to her. Guiding her.

Protecting her.

He shakes his head at the police officer. "Nothing, sorry," he says. "I don't trust my ex's new husband, that's all."

"But it's just a gut feeling, isn't that right, Nate?" Rebecca interjects, her voice jeering at him ever so slightly. Nate ignores her.

"Is there any news?"

"Well, no one has been able to locate Mr. Giovanni or Tabitha, but given there was no sign of forced entry, and Mr. Giovanni's car is gone, it does suggest that he and Tabitha have gone somewhere together. We do understand that Mrs.

Giovanni feels that that is extremely unlikely, but at this stage, I'd suggest waiting until tomorrow to see if this all sorts itself out. These things usually do. Alternatively, if you want to file a missing person's report, we need you to come down to the station." The officer snaps his notebook closed with an air of finality, nodding to his colleague, a silent agreement that it was time for them to go.

"What about the dog?" Rebecca asks, her voice high. She has one arm wrapped around Gen, and Nate moves forward to give his youngest daughter a hug. He strokes her hair and pulls her head onto his chest, murmuring gentle words to her. Gen starts crying quietly again, but Nate can't tell if she's worried about Tabby or if she's crying for Charlie.

"Yes, the dog is concerning." The officer consults his notebook, as though that will help him clarify what has happened here, what the solution might be. But he doesn't add anything else, and Nate grits his teeth.

"What happened last night?" Nate turns to Rebecca, his voice tight. "Did you have a fight? With Tabby? With Leroy? How was she yesterday? Did she seem okay?"

Rebecca's face closes. "She was fine. Wasn't she, Gen? Except..." Here she glances at the officers uneasily. "Apparently she quit her job months ago. But she's been pretending to go every Saturday like usual. Did you know that?" Her tone is accusatory, as though Nate being privy to something she wasn't privy to was the worst thing about that piece of information. She sounds defensive, *and so she should be*, thinks Nate. Saturday is Rebecca's day to look after the kids. *What else was she not keeping track of?*

Nate shakes his head slowly. "So where was she going?" he asks, his eyes conveying the challenge he would never dare to say aloud: *Why weren't you looking after her properly? Why weren't you paying more attention?*

But the police officer interrupts them. "We'll be off now.

But do keep in touch and get back to us if they haven't turned up by tomorrow." He goes to hand Nate a card but Rebecca snatches it out of his hand, her eyes flashing. "Great," she snaps. "Just great. I'm telling you that things were tense between them."

This is news to Nate, and he looks up sharply.

"I am one hundred percent sure they wouldn't go off sightseeing together. And leave their phones and wallets behind. Something is wrong, and isn't it your job to find out what?"

"Whoa, whoa, back up a minute," Nate interjects, nodding to the officers who are heading for the door, despite Rebecca's wrath. He assumes she has discussed this tension with them and their assessment of the situation still stands, so he says, "Thank you, officers. We'll be in touch." Then he turns back to Rebecca. "What's this tension between Leroy and Tab? How long has it been like that? Did something happen?" He knows his suspicions are written all over his face, that Rebecca can see through him, can even probably anticipate the self-satisfied "I told you so" on the tip of his tongue, but he doesn't *want* it to be true. He wouldn't mind being right for once, in this particular relationship, but not about this. Despite his eager jumping on this news, he really does just want to find Tabby and check she's okay.

That she's not fooling around with Leroy, who even Nate has to admit is shockingly good-looking.

Sexy. Alluring.

"It's nothing." Rebecca stares back at him coldly. "He's just been really on board with parenting her, and she resists it, you know? Says he's not her dad. Yada yada yada. Exactly what you'd expect from a sixteen-year-old toward her stepfather setting boundaries."

Nate studies his ex-wife carefully. There's something she's not telling him, but he can't guess what it is. *Is it a subtle dig, that he's not pulling his weight in the parenting department? That Leroy has had to take up the slack?*

"Where is Leroy on Saturdays when Tabby does her vanishing act?" he shoots back, and for a moment he sees a flash of doubt on Rebecca's face. She composes herself instantly though, looking at him pityingly. "My husband is not looking for any extracurricular entertainment, Nathan," she says archly. "We are extremely happy. If you want to know so much about what our daughter gets up to, perhaps you should do a little more with her yourself." And Nate winces, because it's true, he used to have the girls more, he used to have Tabby on Saturdays in fact, but things had come up, life had gotten in the way, and Tabby wasn't even home on Saturdays anyway, so what did it matter if they were at Rebecca's house just one extra day a week? He still had them two days a week, and for most of the holidays.

His thoughts are interrupted though, by a small sob from Genevieve, and Nate realizes with a guilty start that he had forgotten she was even there, listening, and maybe Rebecca was right, maybe he *was* a shit dad.

Who would focus on making accusations rather than comforting their daughter?

"Hey, hey," he says, his face softening, and he reaches for Gen again, pulling her small, compact little frame into his arms. "Let's think about a funeral for Charlie, hey? We'll have it when Tabby's back. But we could make some plans, now. Maybe choose a tree to plant?" Nate's mind is working overtime. He's never been a fan of dogs, but he knows Genevieve is going to need a lot of support over this.

And also, he wouldn't mind taking her out of Rebecca's house and asking a few more questions about what she saw last night.

Not least because he might have been parked outside her house for a good portion of it.

5

When Rebecca gets home from work, Tabby and Freddy are sitting at the kitchen bench, eating pancakes.

"Here, Mrs. G," Freddy says, pushing a plate toward her. Two fluffy pancakes are topped with canned cream, strawberries, and maple syrup. They look delicious.

"You two have certainly perfected your pancakes," she says, smiling, reaching for the plate, and plops herself down on a stool next to her daughter, reaching over to tuck some hair behind Tabby's ear to reveal her face. "Though I'm not sure I'd class this as a wholesome dinner."

"Not dinner, Mrs. G. A snack!" Freddy grins, mopping up the last of her maple syrup with her last bite of pancake. "We will certainly be up for some meat and three veg later, won't we, T?"

Rebecca smiles to herself. She remembers being sixteen, carefree, eating ice cream for morning tea with her besties, never worrying about her weight or how she looked. Her face quickly clouds over, though.

She wasn't always carefree, though, was she?

But she pushes that thought down hastily. She's well-practiced at that particular movement in her psyche.

She smiles over at Freddy, who's almost always the life of the party. Egocentric, sure, but Rebecca enjoys her company, is always encouraging Tabby to invite her over. Recently, it seems they always go to Freddy's house, rather than hers. "What have you been up to, Freddy? How's school? How's life?"

"Can't complain, Mrs. G, can't complain," she responds airily, waving her fork around, then cheekily reaching over and stealing one of Rebecca's strawberries. Rebecca laughs, and pushes her plate across so Freddy has better access.

Freddy looks a bit like Tabby—slim, tall, toned, with long, blonde hair and smooth, tanned skin. Somehow, both of them have embarked on puberty without a single pimple seeming to mark their lovely faces. Now, Rebecca pulls out her phone and indicates she'd like to take a photo. Freddy throws an arm around Tabby expansively and grins at the camera. Tabby seems to shake herself, and gives her mother a tight smile.

"Came home to pancakes made by these two gorgeous creatures" she captions the photo, adding it to her Facebook feed, then snapping it shut.

"What about boys?" Rebecca goes on, teasing. "I hear my girl here might have a thing for a certain Trent, but I can't get a word out of her about it. Maybe you could fill me in?"

Freddy falters ever so slightly, but then smiles brightly. "No boys here, Mrs. G. We're both just busy studying, aren't we, Tab? Don't you worry, I keep an eye on this one, keep her on the straight and narrow." Rebecca thinks she sees something pass between the girls, but it's so subtle she can't quite pin it down.

Is Freddy worried about Tabitha?

"In fact, we're off to do a bit of studying now. Would it be all right if I stayed for dinner, Mrs. G? We'll study for a couple of hours and probably work up a nice big appetite again."

Rebecca smiles her acquiescence, knowing full well that

they'll probably just sit in Tabby's room listening to music and gossiping, but she doesn't mind. Tabby has promised her she'll pick up her grades, that the dip was really nothing, just a lack of motivation for a little while there. Besides, she and Leroy have friends coming over for dinner, and she loves this part of her life: entertaining guests. Interesting conversation. Her successful daughters to show off.

She wonders what Genevieve is up to, and wanders down the hall to check on her.

As usual, she's curled up in bed with a book.

Genevieve always gets great reports, and Rebecca never worries about her achievements or leaving her to be responsible for them herself. She does, however, worry about how quiet her youngest daughter is, how few friends she seems to have. The teachers correct her on this, though—apparently Genevieve is well-liked at school. Quiet, helpful, thoughtful, is how they describe her daughter. Seems to maintain close friends easily.

But Rebecca never sees them.

Genevieve never invites them around to her house.

Without the information from the school, she would have no idea her daughter had any friends at all.

Rebecca startles at this thought, though. Because without the information from the school, she'd had no idea that Tabby's grades were slipping, or that she was possibly seeing a boy, either. There was something back to front about this, something not quite right. Because she was the parent, right? Shouldn't she be telling the school the important things, not the other way around?

What sort of a mother relies on the school for information about her children's lives?

And, more importantly, more concerningly—why don't her daughters share this information with her themselves?

AFTER DINNER, Leroy sits beside Rebecca with one hand resting on her knee.

Freddy has departed, and Tabby and Genevieve have both excused themselves to their rooms.

"What beautiful girls you have," Beth gushes, and Rebecca smiles demurely, though secretly concurring. Tabby had cleared the table for them, and Genevieve had already put the dishwasher on on her way to her room. Her huge mahogany table is decorated with flowers from the garden which Gen had arranged before her guests arrived.

Beth and Sandy are new friends who Rebecca met through tennis. Never a big sports person, she had convinced Leroy that they needed a way to meet new people while also getting a bit of exercise—*it was so hard to find time for everything, why not kill two birds with one stone?*

On the tennis court, Rebecca eyed her husband appreciatively. With his dark skin and messy black hair, he's easily the best-looking man on the courts. He also cycles to work every day, and is in great shape. He loped around the court effortlessly, putting the rest of them to shame.

She's already showed off her handsome husband, and Rebecca is thrilled to now also show off her daughters and her home. She can see the admiration in Beth's eyes as they roam across the tasteful furniture, the spotless presentation. "Tell us about your work, Beth?" she asks now, her blue eyes warm and inviting, and Beth starts to tell her about her dry-cleaning business.

It's certainly not glamorous work, Rebecca thinks to herself, but she had noticed Beth getting out of a Tesla at tennis practice, so it seemed it was lucrative and that Beth and Sandy would be able to provide the type of friendship that Rebecca valued: luxury group holidays, expensive wines. The girls were older now, and could even be left by themselves for a weekend here or there, so she and Leroy could really enjoy themselves.

Beth's sister, Emily, who was also a member of the tennis club and drove a beaten-up old Toyota Echo, had not had an invitation extended to her for dinner.

But she didn't have time for *too* many more friends, Rebecca reasoned. There was a gap left by Rosie, who Rebecca had thought was a good friend, but then they'd had that falling out over the Christmas party. And she wanted to make sure anyone new to the group fitted in, could afford the types of things they did together without making it awkward. She wouldn't say she vetted people, but she was conscious of things like that when making new friends.

Something nags at her about Rosie, an uncomfortable feeling, soft and blurry at the edges, and there's that brief moment where her stomach drops and a thought tries to worm its way in, clouded in self-doubt. But it's foolish, and Rebecca pushes it aside.

Beth's here, isn't she, full of joy and admiration?

Rebecca notices people's admiration.

She doesn't notice how much she needs it to calm her, how much she relies on it.

Anyway, she wants to be friends with people who can contribute something to the group. Not hold the group back.

Her mind wanders. Sandy and Leroy are laughing about something, easy-going, bonding. Beth is talking about her own daughters now, and Rebecca wonders aloud if perhaps they should get the whole family together next time? They talk a little about the perils of parenting teenage girls, the laughter and the wine both flowing, and Rebecca feels contentedness wash though her. Her moment of self-doubt about how little she knew about her daughters' lives has passed. With Beth, she projects so much confidence and competence that she believes in it herself.

Just up the hallway, Genevieve is reading in bed, and in her room, Tabby has pulled out her extensive art supplies. She folds back sketches of Charlie, of Genevieve, her likenesses startling and life-like. She doesn't show them to anyone, not even her sister, though of course Gen has noticed her sketching her from time to time.

Now, she continues working on her latest sketch, in blacks and grays: a man, naked from the waist up, his muscular torso sketched lovingly, his face staring straight at her, eyes heavy with lust.

It's her best work yet, but she can't show anyone, not ever. He's too recognizable—her work is that good.

He's hidden in between one hundred other sketches in her sketch pad, then tucked under the mattress on the trundle underneath her bed, which no one ever uses anymore, since no one—not even Freddy, especially not Freddy—ever stays overnight with her there anymore.

Butterflies cascading in her tummy, she sketches and shades.

6

Nate guides Genevieve through the giant shed to the plants section.

His hand rests lightly on her back.

He and Rebecca had exchanged curt words, but Nate was firm: he thought getting Gen out of the house and doing something productive would help to take her mind off things. At least until they had more information.

His mind, too.

He was torn between driving around like a madman, searching for Leroy's car, but it seemed like searching for a needle in a haystack, when Gen was right there, needing him.

She'd been quiet on the drive, staring out the window vacantly, and Nate hadn't pushed.

"I'm here for you, love, if you want to talk about anything," was all he'd said, and she'd nodded imperceptibly, and they'd driven in silence.

Now, they wander amongst the trees, looking for something special they can plant over Charlie's grave. Eventually Gen stops in front of a magnolia. It's already as tall as Gen, and Nate wonders where on earth it will fit in Rebecca's garden, but he says nothing, and hoists it onto the trolley.

BACK AT THE HOUSE, Rebecca suddenly remembers Tabby's phone, and leaps back to where she left it.

The code doesn't work, though.

Rebecca taps in a few different iterations—any special dates she can think of. Birthdays, mainly. She curses Nate for taking Gen away—Gen might have some more ideas about what to try, but she's reluctant to call Nate to ask over the phone. He might be a bit prissy about invading Tabby's privacy like that.

God knows, invading a person's privacy had certainly got him into enough trouble.

Instead, Rebecca goes to Tabby's room, and looks around, dismayed. She doesn't really know where to start, or what she is looking for. And if she's honest with herself, she's hesitant. She has an indistinct, unsettling fear about what she might find.

But she shakes herself, and opens the wardrobe, her fingers running over Tabby's clothes lightly.

So many nice things.

Rebecca never had such nice things when she was growing up.

She pictures, now, the neat little space she shared with her sister, Moira, and her throat clams up, her heart thumping, and she drags her mind back to this current room, this current problem.

All of Tabby's clothes are hung neatly. There's no mess to sort through; it's easy enough to see all of Tabby's things, because there is no clutter anywhere in this room. Her desk is spotless, a few textbooks stacked uniformly in one corner, the edges all lined up. Her pens and pencils are all inside the penholder, not a single one lying out of place. Opening the drawers, Rebecca finds them in much the same state: neat piles of blank paper, exercise books, staplers, and knickknacks all sitting next to one another in neat lines.

Nothing thrown haphazardly at all.

Something about the orderliness makes her uneasy, but the feeling steals away, tenuous and undefined.

Rebecca has popped in more than she used to, ever since Ms. Paisley raised the slipping grades, but every time Tabby has been sitting dutifully at her desk, pen in hand, earnestly tackling whatever problem her homework consisted of that night. Even when Rebecca peered over her shoulder, there was nothing she saw to ever worry her. And Tabby's grades had started to pick back up.

There was *something*, though. For the first time, Tabby has seemed elusive to Rebecca. She smiles, and nods, and says all the right things, but Rebecca has felt her slipping away. Hiding things. Presenting something on the surface that a mother couldn't snipe about, couldn't argue with, but hiding something beneath it.

Still waters run deep, she thinks to herself, and then thinks, *what a ridiculous saying.* All teenagers brood. All of them hide things from their parents.

Again, something catches in her throat.

Didn't she hide things from her parents?

She shies away from that thought, though.

She barely speaks to her parents these days.

And she certainly never thinks about them. She's not about to start now.

———

WHEN NATE AND GENEVIEVE RETURN, Rebecca is sitting at the kitchen table, her fingers drumming a relentless beat on its surface.

"I found this," she accosts Nate, leaping up and thrusting a piece of paper under his nose before he has even shut the door.

You belong to me, forever, the crumpled paper reads, and Nate looks at Rebecca, questioning.

"It was folded up into a tiny square, tucked into her pillowcase." And Nate raises an eyebrow, taking in the seriousness with which his ex-wife is now conducting herself. Searching for things.

"Who wrote it?" he asks, thinking to himself that whatever Rebecca thinks it is, it really offers nothing concrete for them to go on. Just a boy, in love with his daughter. He hates the thought of anyone staking such a claim on her, but thinks that that bit of paper could mean anything.

Rebecca swivels sharply to face her other daughter. "Do you recognize this writing?" she asks, holding the paper out again.

Genevieve startles, and looks guilty.

She shakes her head, her eyes wide.

"Darling, help us out, please. I know sisters might have secrets. But I'm really worried. Has Tabby been seeing anyone? Trent? Anyone else at school? Who might have written this note?"

For a moment, Nate thinks Gen isn't going to answer at all, but then, ever so softly, she says: "She was seeing Trent for a bit. It was pretty casual. I think Trent liked her more than she liked him, and she had trouble...getting rid of him." Here Gen's eyes widen, and she back-pedals. "I mean, nothing bad. I think he just kept pestering her after she ended things. That's all I know," she adds, a note of defiance in her voice that Nate has never heard before. For all the clichés about teenagers that Tabby lived up to, none of them stood up in regards to Genevieve. Mild-mannered and agreeable, he wonders what the edge in her voice is all about.

"Okay. Right. So we'll let the police know that they should have a chat with Trent. Right now, I need to get into Tabby's phone. Do you know what her passcode is?" Rebecca no longer cares if Nate thinks she is being unreasonable. Her heart is thumping in her chest. She needs information. She needs to *know*.

But here Genevieve looks uneasy again, and Nate and Rebecca both become very still. Independently, they both sense that she has something important to tell them, but she's undecided, she's weighing something up, and they mustn't startle her, mustn't do anything to change her mind.

Seconds tick by, and Genevieve wrestles with something inside herself.

Finally, she says, "Yes. But it won't help you. Because I'm pretty sure she has a second phone."

7

Four-and-a-Half Months Earlier

Tabby sits on her bed, sullen.

She knows Leroy will come back, and she's full of rage.

This time, he hadn't even made it through the door before she'd hissed at him, *"Out, out, out, out, get OUT,"* and he'd gone, thank God.

But she knows he'll be back.

He's trying to make it better. Trying to make it up to her. But he can't make it up to her, and he can't make it better, and she hates him, more than anyone. It's not fair, she can see that. There are plenty of other people she ought to hate more.

Like Trent, who she thought was so sophisticated, at first. He even looked a bit like Leroy, with his black hair and his laughing eyes. But he'd gotten pretty intense, pretty quickly. He wanted to spend every second with her. Every break, every lunch. He started to get jealous when she chatted with other boys. He'd started *manipulating* her. She could see it a mile off, but *why was it so hard to untangle herself from it?* It felt like riding a wave, and she'd caught it, and she just had to go with it, wherever it carried her. It was the path of least resistance. It was so hard to jump off.

It was so familiar.

Just go with it.

Leroy had whispered that to her, once, and she shivers.

Even now, well, she'd broken things off with Trent. She'd enjoyed the sex, to be honest. She felt guilty, dirty even. *What was that about?* Somehow, society's messages about being pure and virginal had crept into her psyche, and she *did* feel sullied, and it was ridiculous.

Anyway, she didn't do any of the things Trent started pushing her to do. They'd only had *normal* sex three times, for God's sake, and he was already pushing for anal, his fingers creeping around to her arse, pulling her cheeks apart, trying to stick a finger in there when she'd already said "no" and she'd been furious, yanked her clothes on and stormed out, shaking.

She knew boys were like this, she had heard girls talking, but it seemed so...degrading. And yet she knew, if she'd really liked him, if she hadn't already been feeling suffocated by him, she probably would have let him, and it would have been all about him, and it would have hurt, and she'd have taken it anyway because that's what you had to do with your boyfriend these days. Half of her friends had done it. Just thinking about it makes her curl over into herself, a physical urge to protect her being, to twist her body up, away from men and their prying eyes, their prying little fingers.

It wasn't like that with *him,* though. And here, finally, Tabitha allows herself a little smile.

Oh, she knew she shouldn't. She knew it was wrong. But it was so nice to be cherished. It was so nice to have someone listen to her, really listen. Someone who could take care of her. Someone who she could rely on, who she could talk to like an adult, who cared about more important things than the things teenage boys cared about.

She had to be careful, though, of course.

She couldn't even tell Freddy.

Secrets only stay secret if nobody knows.

He had bought her a private SIM, and she'd dug out one of her mother's discarded phones, and even though she could never talk about him, never share her dizzying joy with anyone, she could, in private, pull her phone out of its hiding place and read his messages, and grin stupidly to herself.

8

MONDAY

When Freddy finally calls, Nate and Rebecca are sitting together in a state of camaraderie they haven't experienced in years.

Rebecca still couldn't honestly say she knew the reason why Nate had left her. He'd claimed it was all the fighting, but everyone fought, didn't they? It was ridiculous to think you could live for years and years with a person and it be all nice and loving all the time.

It had, of course, driven her on to greater success: a bigger salary, and a new, better-looking husband. She'd kept their house, and done all the renovations that Nate had stalled on for years, and she feels smug whenever he comes over and can see everything he walked away from.

Well, he still has a key. So it's not as though he walked away completely. For a while they even tried to have Sunday dinners together, for the girls' sake. But Rebecca had been simmering with so much hostility and rage, of course it didn't last. It was Gen, in fact, who had said quietly to her one night, "Can we not do family dinners, Mom? Everyone always seems so mad."

Now, Rebecca pounces on her phone.

"Freddy. Darling. What can you tell me? Where might Tabby be?"

Nate can't hear what Freddy has to say, and watches Rebecca closely. Her shoulders are stiff, her eyes laser-focused on something out the front window. She has a pen poised over her pad to take any notes. But as they talk, she slumps.

"Nothing," she says, turning to Nate after she hangs up. "Just what Gen said. She was seeing Trent. He was jealous, possessive. Tabby dumped him and he had trouble accepting it. But there was no one else, as far as Freddy knows. And she didn't know that Tabby had quit Miss Ambrosia, either."

"What about how she was in general? Was she happy? Was anything on her mind? There was that bad patch at school, remember? I wonder if something happened, something that was bothering her..." Nate's voice trails off. He glances carefully at Rebecca. There are certainly some things that he can think of that might bother Tabby.

Rebecca shakes her head. "She said she can't think of anything else that's changed." She shrugs. "I'll call that officer again. Tell them about Trent. Tell them they're still not back and it's not okay. And I guess I better go down to file a report." Here, Rebecca looks at Nate uncertainly, and his heart still jumps a little.

"Of course, I'll come with you. We'd better take Gen, too."

———

AFTER THEY FILE THE REPORT, the three of them troop back into Rebecca's house, somber.

"Do you want me to stay?" Nate asks, hesitantly. He's not thrilled at the thought of leaving Gen here, but equally isn't thrilled at the thought of spending a night back in this house.

Lots of ghosts in the cupboards here.

"No, we'll be fine," Rebecca says, back to being self-contained, in control. Breezy, almost. She'd keel over and die before she admitted she needed anything from Nate.

But Gen looks worried. "Can I stay with Dad?" she asks, not quite looking at Rebecca, trepidation in her eyes. She doesn't elaborate and Nate bites his tongue, waits for Rebecca to respond first.

Rebecca hesitates. "Maybe it would be best if you stayed here, Nate. If it's not too much trouble. So we're all together, we can share information."

"Sure," he says, trying to sound casual. "I've got some spare clothes in the car. Let's get some take-away and try to get some rest."

As he turns to the stack of menus near the fridge, exactly where they used to be, a strange feeling settling in his stomach, a phone pings, though, and they all freeze.

Rebecca pounces on Tabby's phone, and a message flashes up from an unknown number.

They stare at it in silence, shocked.

Dirty slut.

9

FOUR MONTHS Earlier

Freddy and Tabby are lounging on Freddy's bed, their long, brown legs stretched out in front of them. Donk, Freddy's Burmese cat, purrs half-heartedly beside Tabby, and she strokes his soft fur absentmindedly.

Both girls are scrolling through their Instagram and TikTok feeds, occasionally showing each other something that makes them laugh.

"You're awfully quiet today," Freddy ventures.

In fact, Tabby has been quiet for a while, and even Freddy's mother, Nancy, has noticed. Privately, Nancy worries about Freddy's friendship with Tabby. She actively encourages Freddy to socialize with some of her other friends—bright, bubbly ones who bring joy and laughter into the house...unlike Tabby, who seems almost morose these days. But Freddy insists that Tabby is her best friend, and in her more generous moments, Nancy thinks it's a good thing that Freddy can support her through whatever she's going through. She's happy that her daughter has such loyalty. When Freddy was younger, Nancy would have fully expected her to ditch a friend who became dull. She seemed perpetually distracted by the next shiny thing, and Nancy worried equally about such frivolousness.

Now, Nancy pokes her head in the door.

"You girls need anything?"

Freddy rolls her eyes. "Mo-om," she reprimands her mother. "You're supposed to knock!"

"Sorry, sweetie." Nancy smiles apologetically at her daughter. "I'm going to make some rocky road. You want to help?"

"No," says Freddy, at the same time that Tabby says, "Yes."

Freddy rolls her eyes again, but follows Tabby out to the kitchen, where Tabby perches on a barstool, intermittently asking Nancy for instructions.

She doesn't talk at all otherwise, and Nancy glances from one girl to the other surreptitiously.

Are they fighting? she wonders. But Tabby seems distracted, rather than upset. And Nancy had definitely heard them laughing just before she stuck her head in Freddy's door.

The girls have lounged on these barstools more times than Nancy can remember. They used to be louder, though, more joyful, and Nancy relishes this opportunity to watch them, to try to figure out what's going on.

It always seemed an unlikely friendship to her. On the surface, sure, she could see the attraction. Both pretty and sporty, they'd been popular at school, popular with the girls *and* the boys. Tabby always outshone Freddy just slightly at everything, though. She was beautiful, where Freddy was merely pretty; she was top of the class, whereas Freddy hovered in the top five or six.

For all that, Nancy glowed with pride whenever she thought about her only child. Freddy was honest, strong-willed, smart. But more than that, she was a problem-solver. She had robust self-esteem and bounced back from setbacks. While other mothers fretted about eating disorders and their daughters capitulating to peer pressure or the lusts of boys, Nancy was always startled by Freddy's diplomacy, her resilience, her ability to get on with things. When there'd been fallouts in the friendship group—just normal teenage girl bitchiness, to be honest—it was Freddy who offered support, who smoothed things over. Even when she herself felt hurt or left out, she dealt with it so maturely. She'd talk to Nancy about it, but she always had a positive outlook, a sensible approach. And sure, sometimes Nancy gave herself a pat on the back about that—she definitely tried to cultivate that in her approach to parenting—but she also thinks that it is just who her daughter is. She's not worried in the least about what grades Freddy finishes school with. She has no doubt her daughter will find a corner of the world to thrive in, and she can't wait to see what she does with her life.

Now, she watches Tabby stir the melted chocolate through the nuts and marshmallows. She seems ephemeral, too beautiful for this Earth, and too distant. But for all her success and beauty, Nancy gets the feeling that it is Tabby who leans on Freddy, not the other way around.

What does someone so outwardly perfect have to worry about?

She hopes to God that Tabby doesn't get mixed up in anything unsavory, because however smart Freddy might be, she seems to be bonded to Tabby with such strength that it might drag Freddy down, rather than pull Tabby out.

"How are you finding school this year, Tab?" Nancy asks now, rifling through cupboards for an appropriate tin, careful not to look directly at Tabby. She's always found that conversations with teenagers work best when you're not looking at them.

"S'okay," Tabby says, not looking up. Despite volunteering to help, Tabby seems uncomfortable to Nancy. But she keeps trying.

"Do you still see much of the other girls? We haven't seen

them much, have we, Freddy? Lisa and Mona and Cate? What are they up to these days?"

Tabby is silent, and Freddy jumps in: "We hang with them at school, don't we Tabby? Cate's seeing Peter, though, so she's always hanging out with him on the weekends. And without her organizing stuff to do, we just sort of stopped doing it. We should try to organize something. Maybe next weekend I'll organize a movie night. Could we do it here, Mom?"

"Of course," Nancy says, relieved. She would love to see all the girls together again, just check how they're all going, how Freddy is with them. She loves Freddy's friends, she really does, but also she just wants to make sure Freddy doesn't put all her eggs in one basket, so to speak. Especially when that one basket seems a bit sketchy of late.

"How's your mom, Tabby? How's Genevieve?"

Here Tabby looks up, and stares blankly at Nancy. For a second, Nancy thinks she sees the hint of a sneer, but then Tabby looks back down and mixes the rocky road ingredients with renewed vigor, her little shoulders rigid with tension that Nancy can't understand.

Later, she'll ask Freddy if Tabby and her mother or sister fight, and Freddy will shake her head, shrugging. "Just the usual with her mom. Every now and then. But Tabby hates fighting, she's always really sad if there's a fight."

"Well, we all hate fighting, I think," Nancy muses. "And it's hard being a teenager. With her dad not there, too. She just seemed a bit quiet here the other day. I hope everything is okay with her." Nancy is careful not to pry, and leaves a quiet space for Freddy to raise anything, but Freddy seems oblivious, and goes on chatting about other things, and Nancy files her observations away, and gets on with her day.

10

When Nate wakes up on Tuesday, he's momentarily disoriented.

He's in the spare room, in the same bed he used to sleep in when things started to go downhill between Rebecca and him. The same picture taunts him from the far wall. The same slash of sunlight creeps in and dazzles him through a gap in the blinds and the wall, which he could never successfully block off, waking him twenty minutes earlier than he wanted to be woken.

Memories rush in through that crack in the blinds, too, burnt into his mind, resurfacing, however much he tries to bury them.

Guilt, mainly.

He pushes them aside though, and swings his legs out of the bed.

He's a heavy sleeper, and he wants to check that Tabby and Leroy didn't return while he was sleeping.

He feels a momentary pang of guilt. His daughter is missing, and he slept like he had no cares in the world.

Was something wrong with him?

Padding down the hall to Tabby's room, he sees that Rebecca has had the same thought. She's standing in the doorway, and startles when she sees him. She gives a barely perceptible shake of her head.

No Tabby, then.

They'd called the number from the message, of course. Genevieve had gone white, but she'd entered the passcode—one-zero-zero-six. One thousand and six. The tenth of June. October 2006. *What did it represent?*

But it had gone straight to a recorded message, "the person you have called is not available," and then a dial tone. There was no option to leave a message. And there was no record of any texts or phone calls to or from that number in Tabby's phone. Google showed up nothing, and the police hadn't been able to trace it, either.

They'd searched her room methodically then, not speaking. Trying to find her second phone, while Gen sat resolutely in front of the television, which was off, stony-faced. "We're just trying to find her," Nate had said, gently, but Genevieve wouldn't even look at him, and he couldn't quite work out what she was angry about. *That they were invading Tabby's privacy? That she wouldn't want them to invade hers?*

He knows he should talk to her, explain it or explore it or something, but he can't concentrate on all these different threads at once. He just needs to focus on finding Tabby. Then he'll have a better talk with Gen.

Of course it made more sense that Tabby had taken her other phone with her, and left this one behind. *If you had a secret phone, that's the one you'd keep with you, right?*

That's if she went of her own accord, of course. If it was well-hidden, and she went against her will...

Nate had stiffened at that thought, though, and pushed it aside, too. He can't tolerate thinking about worst-case scenarios, and consciously lets his mind skip away from them. Being paralyzed by terror isn't going to help him find his daughter.

Now, he nods at Rebecca, an acknowledgement.

It's been twenty-four hours.

Something is very, very wrong.

And he's not sure that he and Rebecca are the people best-placed to make it right.

Somehow, a missing daughter throws everything into stark relief. All the things he's successfully not thought about for years loom large in his mind. All the things he and Rebecca have gotten wrong, have buried. *Of all the times these thoughts could rush to the surface, try to claw their way into his consciousness, why now, when he is least prepared, when he is so poorly placed to deal with them?* he wonders.

He just wants to find Tabby.

And he can't quite make the link that problems in the past might be related to problems in the present.

The police have not been very helpful. As far as they're concerned, Tabby is sixteen. Nate and Rebecca can hate it all they like, but legally, Tabby is over the age of consent. She can run off with Leroy if she wants to.

But what if she didn't want to?

Even the dog, they just shrugged. Was he killed, or did he have a heart attack?

There're no bodies, no evidence of foul play. Only Rebecca's insistence that Leroy and Tabby weren't really getting along, and they would never have gone off together voluntarily.

Nate wonders how much he can trust Rebecca's judgment, though. She doesn't have the greatest track record of emotional intelligence when it comes to family matters.

Does he, though?

"Walk me through it again," he says now, to Rebecca. "Sunday night. Sunday afternoon, even. Try to remember everything."

Any other day, Rebecca would have told him to go to hell. But today, their daughter and her husband are missing, and she can't think of anything else to do so early on a Tuesday morning.

"Let's get coffee," Nate says, and she follows him obediently to the kitchen, and he marvels again at all the different Rebeccas she manages to keep inside her skin.

———

"WE DID HAVE A FIGHT."

Nate looks up from his half-empty coffee, the movement sharp, but his expression careful.

Rebecca had given him the run-down: it had been a quiet day. They'd had friends over the night before, so they were a bit hungover. Genevieve had spent nearly all day in bed, reading. They were having a weird cold snap, not that unusual in Melbourne at this time. But they were all a bit lethargic.

Tabby had been studying. Her year ten final exams were only a week away. She'd been working hard, with little prompting from Rebecca.

Rebecca had been gardening, half-heartedly. Leroy had spent the morning reading the paper, and then had gone to the markets to get food for a roast.

She left out that she and Leroy had bickered a little—there were leftovers from the night before. She's always extravagant when they have guests. There's always leftovers. And Rebecca thought cooking more food was a waste of time and money. She wanted Leroy to help her in the garden. After he'd gone, she pulled weeds out with unusual ferocity, muttering to herself.

So she was in a bad mood. She can see that. But what follows her bad moods is always less clear to her. It's uncomfortable, and blurry, and she shuts it down, often with the same phrase, and she never looks more closely at it, and she never tries to change it, and sitting opposite her, Nate doesn't even need her to tell him anymore, he can imagine it exactly, can see it perfectly clearly in his mind's eye, and he shrivels inside a little bit, because he knows this story, he knows it so well, and yet he did nothing, nothing, nothing, to make it better.

He takes a deep breath, though, and is just about to ask more questions, when Rebecca says, "It was nothing. She disrespected me. I shouted a bit, and she went to her room. She said some awful things. I would have left her. But Leroy went to see if she was all right. I went to bed. And when I woke up, they were gone."

11

THE GIRL SITS on her bed quietly.

She can hear her parents arguing, trying to maintain hushed voices in their room. Occasionally one of them forgets, their voices rising to an exaggerated hiss with sharp edges and pointy inflections, which carry easily to her.

Their bedroom is not so far from hers.

She tries to do the right thing. She tries to help, to be useful. She offers to babysit her younger sister, and make dinner, even to brush her mother's hair.

She's always getting it wrong somehow, though.

This afternoon, her mother had just looked through her, as though she didn't exist, and she wonders what it is she did wrong, this time. Did she not put her breakfast bowl in the sink? She knows she spilt the milk, but she is sure she cleaned it up and there was no mess left, none at all, she is sure of it.

She must have done something wrong, though, and if she could just work it out, if she could just try a bit harder, she knows that she could please her mother, and her parents would stop fighting, and they could be happy, and go to the park, like the families she sees out the car window when they drive to the supermarket.

They drive past, and they never stop.

At least, they used to. Now, they don't even take her to the supermarket. Sometimes, she'll leave her bedroom and find that they are gone. When she asks later, timidly, where they went, they'll tell her the supermarket, and seem not to even notice that their children might be afraid, left at home alone.

She tries so hard. And it's not easy to be the best at everything, at school, at home. But if she just tries harder, if she just does her very best, she knows she can make them happy, and her mother will smile at her, and hold her, and laugh with her in bed on Saturday mornings, and everything will be okay.

Now, she rises quietly from her bed. She starts to order the things in her room, folding clothes that she'd left on the floor, placing them neatly back in drawers. It doesn't matter if they're clean or dirty, so long as the floor is clean, everything put away in its place.

She wipes down her desk with a tissue, neatly lining up her pencils, and when everything is perfect, she slips into bed with her sister, who is huddling under the covers, blocking out the anger, the fight, the coldness in their home.

She slips in beside her and wraps her arms around her and wonders what else she can do to be her very best self, and make her mother happy.

12

THREE-AND-A-HALF MONTHS EARLIER

Tabby skips home from school with more joy in her step than Genevieve has seen in a long time.

She, Genevieve, is dragging her feet. Her mother's new friends are coming round for dinner tonight, and Genevieve doesn't mind helping with dinner, she really doesn't. It's the talking that she minds. The false smiles, pretending everyone is happy. Fielding all the interested questions, having to participate. Having to get to know someone new.

Again.

Oh, Beth seems perfectly lovely. But she's bringing her own daughters tonight, girls that Genevieve has never met, and she'll have to be friendly, she'll have to be attentive, she'll have to pretend that they're all going to be great friends, that they'll have a future together, when surely everyone knows that is not going to happen?

Well, Beth doesn't know. She saw the way Beth was looking at her mother last month, the fawning eyes, her feeling of sheer luck that she'd managed to befriend someone so sophisticated, so fun, so successful.

When Rebecca makes new friends, they feel like they have won the lottery.

Genevieve has seen it all before. And she's lost friends, too, people she really actually *did* care about, from previous times that she's done this dance. The Happy Family Dance, she calls it.

She's done it enough times to give it a name.

She misses Rosie and the twins. They used to visit all the time, even go on holidays together. The twins were Gen's age, and it was the only time Gen didn't feel like the third wheel, following her older sister around. When the twins were there, Genevieve was the center of attention, and it wasn't so much that she liked that, more that it made her feel carefree. Like she didn't have to look out for Tabby, make sure Tabby wasn't getting sick of looking after her little sister.

She doesn't know why they stopped visiting, though she could take a pretty good guess.

Now, she drags her feet, and wonders why Tabby seems so chipper.

"Beth tonight," she says, watching her sister from sideways eyes, and Tabby does a double take.

"Oh yeah," she says. But her stride only dampens down for a minute or two. Then she's skipping ahead again, a small smile playing around her lips.

"Why are you so cheerful? It's been nearly two weeks. The clock is ticking."

Tabby stops dead in her tracks. She turns to face her sister. Something flickers across her face.

Guilt?

"Listen, Gen," she says, leaning down, taking her sister by the shoulders and looking earnestly into her eyes. "We're not stuck at home forever, you know? It feels like it, when things are bad. It feels like that's all of life. But we're growing up. We'll have other things, other people. Don't forget that, okay? If, when I'm gone..." Here she trails off, and Genevieve has a moment of fear.

"Where are you going?" And when Tabby is silent, a distant look in her eyes: "Are you going somewhere, Tab?"

"No, of course not." Tabby shakes herself, as though to get rid of her troubling thoughts. "I just mean, you know. You'll be there without me, when I finish school. And I know it's never been about you, and I hope it never becomes about you. And you can call me, any time, you know. Wherever I am, twenty years from now, you can call me if you need me. I just... It's finally seeming like there's an end in sight, you know?" And here Tabby lurches forward suddenly, hugging Genevieve to her tightly, her voice choked.

"I love you, Gen. I'll always look out for you, you know that, right?"

Then she spins around and starts walking quickly away.

Genevieve stays where she is.

Is Tabby wiping away tears? she wonders, watching Tabby's retreating back. She has a slightly sick feeling deep in her abdomen. There's something Tabby isn't telling her. And if Tabby is leaving (*where would she go? To Nate's house? To Freddy's? Is she going to run away?*), then the carefully balanced life Genevieve tiptoes around—never disrupting, never rocking the boat—seems suddenly, terrifyingly, very unbalanced and very unsafe.

WHEN THE GIRLS walk in the front door, Rebecca greets them with a big smile and a giant pile of flowers.

"Genevieve, darling, would you work your magic on these flowers for me? You'll meet Beth's daughters for the first time tonight, I want to make them feel welcome, like we're excited to see them, so they know that we're going to some effort to welcome them into our lives."

"Of course," says Genevieve, reaching out to touch the stems, see what's there. Already imagining how to fit them together. She has a knack for making things beautiful. The process itself is like a meditation, staring at the shock of color, the extravagance of nature. Taking the time to make the arrangement just so.

When she's finished, she'll stare at her work, stare at it and stare at it, and wish she could arrange the rest of her life just so, too.

You want to make them feel welcome, or you want to make them feel envious of your perfect life?

No one would ever guess that's what she's thinking beneath her calm demeanor, the eager way her hands reach toward the flowers, lovingly touching and sorting them, selecting each stem for the arrangement so that it is perfect, too. Her expression—also perfected, over the years—is one of sweetness and generosity. Rebecca would have no idea what's underneath it.

"Good girl, thank you," Rebecca says now, turning her attention back to an impressive array of ingredients on the bench. She's humming to herself, cheerful, consumed with the task at hand.

The Happy Family Dance.

Even Leroy is in a good mood. He wanders into the kitchen, whistling, and pulls Rebecca to him with a grin, kissing her on the lips, one hand creeping down to feel her ass. She swats his hand away.

"Afternoon, girls," he says, smiling over at Gen, then Tabby. "How was school?"

"Fine, thank you," Gen says, distracted. Beth and her daughters are an annoyance, but it's Tabby's strange little speech that she's thinking about. But she's yanked out of her thoughts by Tabby's reply.

Panic rises in her chest in step with Tabby's words. As soon as she hears the first one, the tone of it, she's hurled into confusion. *What is Tabby doing? Wasn't she just in a perfectly good mood, even if she was making strange noises about being gone?*

"Better than being fucking here," is what Tabby says, and flounces off to her room, and it's so out of character, it's not how they manage this, it's not how this family works, *why would she do this?*

Everything in the kitchen seems to slow down. Even Tabby's door slamming down the hall is extended, drawn out, the noise rising in Gen's ears long after the door is firmly shut. Rebecca's face slams shut too, a tight little expression all that remains, but Leroy is back next to her immediately, his voice soothing, his arm quick to wrap around his wife. From the outside, anyone would think he was comforting her, lamenting the rudeness of her daughter.

Only Genevieve can see that he is actually holding her back.

13

TUESDAY

"I was at the house Sunday night."

Nate's heart is hammering in his chest. He keeps his eyes fixed on the road.

He's driving with Rebecca, choosing places that Leroy or Tabby frequent, looking, honestly, for God knows what. Leroy's car. An idea. A clue.

Genevieve refused to come. Nate was surprised that she'd stay in the house by herself, but she was adamant, and he can hardly blame her. Spending time with Nate and Rebecca together has not been a comfortable experience in a long, long while.

"What?"

Nate can feel Rebecca staring at him, her mind ticking over, trying to place this piece of information somewhere useful.

"I heard something. Look, I don't really know what I was thinking. Or what I heard. But..." His words trail off. On Sunday night, he'd felt foolish. Now, with Tabby and Leroy missing, he knows he needs to come clean to Rebecca, but he feels defensive and worried. *Might he have been the last person to see Leroy? And if he was sort of, maybe, spying on him...where does that fit in a missing persons investigation?*

"The girls were with me on Wednesday night. And I ordered pizza. And when I came back in, they obviously hadn't heard me. So I'm standing in the hallway taking my coat off, juggling bloody boots and pizza boxes, and I can hear some sort of argument. And you know they never argue, they're so sweet together. And I wasn't eavesdropping, but I was just shocked, you know? So I just froze. It was so unexpected. They seemed fine when I went out, just normal, you know? And I only heard a few words before I called out. But then those words just really bothered me, and I thought about them all week, and my mind was going a bit crazy, you know—"

"Just spit it out, Nate! What did you hear?" Rebecca is exasperated, but also on edge, and Nate's words are tumbling over each other, his palms clammy. He doesn't know if he should be telling Rebecca this or not.

"Tabby was hissing at Gen, like low and angry. She said 'Mind your own fucking business.' And Gen sounded really upset, she said, 'He's way too old for you, Tabby! It's disgusting! How could you do that to...' And God, I wish I hadn't called out. I wish I heard who Tabby is supposed to be doing this bad thing to. But I felt like it was not appropriate to be listening. But now she's gone and—"

"For fuck's sake, Nate! Since when have you been all high and mighty about being appropriate? And you assumed the old guy is Leroy, of course." Rebecca is rigid with anger, her teeth clamped together between words so hard that Nate thinks it must be making her jaw ache. He steals glances at her, taking deep slow breaths, trying to calm himself.

"There was *one incident,* Rebecca. One fucking incident in *forty years* where I was inappropriate. Isn't it time you let that go? Especially since—" Here he stops himself though. Now is not the time to get into that. They've never seen eye to eye on that particular topic, and it's not worth arguing about now.

"So why were you at the house? Did you really think you'd see something inappropriate in my front garden? Even *if* the 'too old' man is my husband—*which it's not*—what exactly did you think you'd spy on Sunday night?"

"Well, actually. I just tried to ask the girls casually, you know, what they were up to for the weekend. Didn't let on I'd heard anything." Here Rebecca rolls her eyes, but Nate ignores her. He was sure he'd pulled it off. Casual inquiries, no ulterior motive. "And Tabby said she was catching up with a friend on Sunday night. And Gen looked really upset when she said that. And I just thought I might see where she came home from. Which direction. If anyone dropped her off. If she seemed especially happy, or something. Anything, really. And yes, if you must know, if Leroy arrived home ten minutes later or something suspicious like that. I know you think it's stupid, but she's been weird all year. And you're so caught up in—"

"Oh, fuck off, Nate," Rebecca says, her voice cold. "You're being a jerk, for a change. You'd love it, wouldn't you? My new husband to prefer our daughter. You're disgusting. And you're wrong. Leroy was home all night. With me. And as far as I know, Tabby was with Freddy."

They're both silent. Then at the same time they both start: "But Fred said—" They don't need to finish the sentence. Fred had said they hadn't seen Tabby all weekend.

"Fuck." Rebecca slams her hands on the console in front of her. "Well, she came home when she said she would. Did you see that?"

"Yes. She rode her bike in at about ten. It was too dark for me to see much, but she seemed calm. Not in a rush, or worried, or agitated or anything."

"I don't think she *told* me she was meeting Freddy. I don't think she lied about it. I think I just assumed, because she doesn't seem to see anyone else these days." Rebecca seems defeated, all the fight and anger gone out of her. For a moment, Nate feels almost sorry for her. *Has she really not noticed how reserved Tabby has become? How different from the child he remembers when they were together?*

Here, Nate winces, though. *Because he has had something to do with that, hasn't he?*

Rebecca might not have noticed, but Nate has. *And what, exactly, has he done to help his eldest daughter or even talk to her about what he's noticed?*

For the longest time, he's thought that it would work itself out, that he didn't really need to do anything, but now he wonders whether Tabby is missing precisely because he did nothing.

He could take a guess at why Tabby is so quiet. And he did absolutely nothing to help her.

Nate hesitates.

He wonders how much he should tell Rebecca. If, for instance, he should share his theory about what was going wrong for Tabby. If he should share with her Tabby's solution to the problem.

If he should tell her how long he sat outside her house.

And who else he saw out there.

As he weighs how much to share with Rebecca, though, her phone rings, and as she listens to the person on the other end, her face goes white.

The phone slips from her fingers, sliding underneath her seat, a tinny, distant voice calling out indistinctly from under there, and Nate thinks he is going to vomit, wrenching the steering wheel into a crooked park on the sidewalk, his breath coming in little gasps.

"Bec. Bec. What? What is it?" His words are urgent, he's fumbling for her phone underneath her seat, wanting to know but not wanting to know, and she breathes out, her voice empty and distant: "They've found Leroy. He's dead."

14

THREE MONTHS Earlier

"You're not exactly helping yourself, though, are you?"

Leroy is trying to look patient, but Tabby can sense his frustration.

He came into her room a few minutes ago, locking the door behind him. The lock is new. When she'd looked at it, then looked back at him, he hadn't quite met her eyes.

Was he just subtly letting her know there was a lock there now? Without having to spell it out to her?

God forbid they should talk about it.

"Look, your mom's under a lot of pressure at work. She's trying to wrap up a big project. She just needs a little understanding and cooperation from you. But it's like you're *trying* to upset her, and I don't understand. Why would you do that, Tab?" He comes and sits on her bed, edges closer to her, and she remembers all the times he's done exactly the wrong thing, and feels overcome with rage.

"You keep coming in here, thinking you have some right, thinking you can help, but have you ever helped, Leroy? Or have you just made things worse?"

Even a few short months ago, it would have been inconceivable to Tabby to talk to Leroy this way. But things have changed, now. She's buoyed up by love. She can see other options, a future, and anything less than honesty and action feels like a betrayal.

Leroy claims to love her, but what has he ever done but make it worse?

"I try to help." Leroy falters, looking worried. "I thought I was helping. What do you actually want me to do, Tab? I'm just trying to keep everyone happy."

"No." Tabby shakes her head emphatically. "No, you're not, Leroy. Stop lying to yourself, and to me. You're trying to keep Rebecca happy. Not me. Not Genevieve. And you can't do both. You have to choose. Me, or Rebecca. You can't keep us both happy, do you understand?"

Leroy looks shocked, like he genuinely hasn't realized this, and Tabby wonders how stupid he thinks she is, or how stupid he might in fact be himself. She can feel power coursing through her, and it's a revelation to her that she can be powerful, that she can say things and decide things and have some control over things. She would never have thought this possible. In fact, she's been doing the exact opposite of this and she now feels sorry for that girl, the Tabitha of two, three, four months ago, who huddled in her room and let things happen to her. Who crept around and tried so hard to do everything right. It was *sensational*, to do something so different. To stop trying. To make mess, instead of perfection. And what difference did it actually make to the outcome? Leroy would still slink into her room, she would still feel terrible and afraid—but that all happened whether she cooperated or not. So she might as well complain, loudly.

Now, she sits up straight, looks Leroy in the eye. "Get out of my room, Leroy," she says. And as he stands to leave, dithering, one hand on the door, she adds, "And tell my mother to go to hell."

15

In the car, Rebecca is howling.

Awkwardly leaning over the center console, Nate tries to comfort her, and she turns her face into his shoulder, her tears wetting his tee shirt in moments.

Gingerly, he strokes her hair.

"I need to identify the body. There's no ID. But his car was there and the description matches. They want a formal statement." Rebecca is hiccupping softly between words, her face still buried in Nate's shoulder. She seems fragile, and childlike, a state that he can only remember seeing Rebecca in once before. When she told him about her sister.

After that one time, she had banned them discussing the topic ever again.

Now, Nate is torn between tenderness, a little tiny green shoot of something still alive regarding his feelings for Rebecca, and fear. For his daughter.

For them all.

Was Leroy abusing her? Did she finally snap, and retaliate?
Or was it something worse?

"Let's go to the station. Or, where? Where do they want you?"

"Forensic Medicine. Then the station. I'll direct you." Already Rebecca is pulling herself together, straightening her shoulders, getting back in charge.

"We need to get Gen." Nate suddenly remembers his youngest daughter, alone in the house. His heart starts hammering in his chest, and he shoves the car back into drive, screeching off the curb without waiting for Rebecca to agree with him.

Gen. Jesus.

He tries to think about how Gen will take this news. On top of Charlie. She'll be terrified.

Did she love Leroy? Will she be devastated? Nate tries to remember how Gen related to her stepfather. He was too busy worrying about Leroy leering at Tabby to pay much attention. And he was certainly still caught up in his own complicated feelings about Rebecca moving on to be able to offer any objective guidance on how to navigate a blended family.

In amongst his fears as he belts back toward Rebecca's house that familiar emotion starts to surface again, though.

Guilt.

Because if he is very honest about it, if he doesn't hide anything from himself, the thing that bubbles to the surface is the knowledge, crystal clear, that he knew that his girls were not all right, and he did absolutely nothing to help them.

NATE IS surprised by how calm Rebecca is after identifying Leroy's body.

Nate himself had waited in reception, Gen slumped on him, alternately sobbing and staring blankly at the wall. She has said not a single word.

On the way from Forensic Medicine to the police station they are all quiet. Rebecca stares out the window, her face blank, her posture defeated. Nate thinks she's in shock, and she shouldn't be making a statement to police in this state, but ever-efficient, she wants to take action. She wants to find answers. She's always been better at doing than feeling.

Nate's mind wanders back to that conversation about Moira. It was the only time he'd ever seen Rebecca out of control with pain. He's certainly seen her out of control with anger, but that day she had sobbed and sobbed, her mouth hanging open, her eyes wild. But just as quickly she'd dried her tears.

"I don't want to talk about it," she'd said. And then, emphatically: "Ever again."

Nate thinks perhaps he fell in love with her more that day. It was like he'd been allowed in, to something private and painful; he was trusted. And it's hard not to move toward someone in pain, it was human nature, wasn't it? When you share painful things, you grow closer.

In his more cynical moments, since separating, he'd wondered if it was all contrived. Theatre, for what purpose? To pull him in closer? To create the illusion of intimacy? Because he certainly never felt that close or that trusted in their marriage, ever again. He'd tried. Tried to talk about it, to understand it, to see if Rebecca really truly didn't want to talk about it, or if it was something festering that burying only made worse, not better. But Rebecca had only gotten angry. It seemed that she really, truly, did not want to talk about it ever again.

He'd tried, hadn't he?

He drags his thoughts back to Leroy. He was found in the Yarra River. His car was near the Tandy Bridge. Nate's first thought was that it was an embarrassing place to die. It was a humble little bridge, there was nothing impressive about it. *Did he jump? Was he pushed?*

It wasn't even that high. Why didn't he swim?

"They'll have more answers after the autopsy," Rebecca had told him, her voice soft. "And after forensics go through his car."

But of course, Tabby has been in Leroy's car. He drives her places. She was learning to drive with Leroy. Nate still remembers the stab of jealousy he'd felt when she'd told him.

How will forensics work out if she was in his car on Sunday night? If she struggled? If he held her against her will? Nate thinks he is going to be sick.

What if Leroy didn't take Tabby?

What if it was someone else?

In which case, where is she now?

He pulls in to the police station and takes deep breaths.

Then he flings open his door and vomits on the asphalt.

A DETECTIVE OFFERS Rebecca tissues and tea, studying her carefully.

Rebecca is poised, her face neutral. She doesn't look like someone who has just lost her husband.

"I'm Detective Casey. I'm so sorry about your husband, Mrs. Giovanni. Divers are in the river now, looking for evidence."

Neither of them mention what they're both thinking —*looking for Tabby.*

"Are you sure you want to make your statement now? Do you want anyone with you, to support you? A lawyer?"

"Why would I need a lawyer?" Rebecca looks genuinely surprised, like the thought had not even crossed her mind.

"You don't, necessarily. But this may be a homicide investigation. Some people might call a lawyer."

Rebecca waves a hand dismissively. "I just want to get it

done. I want to find Tabby. I want to feel like I'm doing something."

"Okay. Well, thank you for coming down. I appreciate this is a very difficult time and we will do everything we can to find your daughter as soon as possible. Anything you can tell me to shed light on the events leading up to the disappearance might help. So why don't you go over the twenty-four hours before they went missing."

Rebecca goes over what she told Nate, with a few extra details. Beth and Sandy came for dinner on the Saturday night; they were a bit hungover on Sunday. She and Leroy bickered.

The girls were in their rooms most of the day.

She and Tabby had fought.

"What about?" Casey is watching Rebecca kindly, her eyes warm and attentive. She notes the way Rebecca's face closes off.

"It was nothing. Just normal teenage stuff. She said something disrespectful. I shouted at her. I shouted too much. It was out of proportion. I just get sick of her lip, you know?"

Casey doesn't know. She doesn't have children. She doesn't even have nieces or nephews. But she's heard enough from friends to have an idea of what Rebecca is referring to.

"Do you fight often?"

"No. Not really. We have words maybe once a month, just normal teenage pushing boundaries stuff. If her grades are bad. If she's disrespectful. It's been a bit worse than usual the last few months. I don't know what's gotten into her."

"I see. And have there been any other changes? A boyfriend? Any other stresses? School work, or illness, or peer trouble?"

"No. She was seeing a boy—I gave the other officer his name—about six months ago, and her grades started slipping, but she ended things with him. Apparently, he was quite possessive and didn't take the breakup well, so you should talk to him for sure. But after that, her grades picked back up, she seemed settled. Having her friends over less, but that makes sense, she was studying for her year ten finals. Although—" Rebecca trails off, her eyes distant. *Wasn't she noticing that Tabby was quieter than before?*

"Yes?" Casey prompts.

"She was maybe a bit quieter than usual. Keeping to herself more. She was always popular, you know? Sporty, smart, lots of friends. And I think recently she's been spending a lot more time alone. And then." Rebecca hesitates again, not wanting to admit that she didn't know about quitting Miss Ambrosia. "Well, she worked Saturdays at this café. And when I called them, they said she'd quit months ago. But she's been pretending to me she was still going there every week." Rebecca shrugs, not quite meeting the detective's eyes.

"And what about Leroy? How were things with him? Between you? Did he have anyone he was fighting with?"

Rebecca hedges and avoids. *Things were fine. Weren't they? They were bloody fine.*

They were *mostly* fine, but there was that fight, that *one* fight, when Tabby was so bloody crazy, and Leroy, the way he looked at her, like *she* was the crazy one.

The way he looked at her, but instead of coming to *her,* he gave her that awful, awful look, and followed Tabby to her room, and *locked the bloody door.*

16

WHEN THE LITTLE girl is a bit older, her mother enrolls her in swimming lessons.

"You learn, and then you can teach your sister," she says, pushing the girl impatiently into the pool.

The water is cold, and the girl has never been in a pool before. An instructor with a friendly smile beckons her over to the group, and the girl tries to go to her, but it's too deep, and her feet can't touch the bottom.

Panicking, she windmills her arms furiously, the coldness knocking her breath out of her, the water terrifying, and she can't breathe, and she starts sinking, and she doesn't know what to do.

Then strong arms are pulling her up, the instructor's face now worried, waving at a colleague to watch the other children, looking around for her mother, who is nowhere to be seen.

"Honey, this class is for nine-year-olds who've completed the other classes. Have you done the other classes?"

The girl shakes her head, feels like a failure.

"It's my first time," she whispers.

"Your first lesson?" The instructor sounds incredulous, but the girl shakes her head.

"My first time in a pool."

"Where are you parents?" The instructor sounds angry now, and the girl feels even worse: she shouldn't be here, she's done something wrong again, she's in the way, she's wasting people's time.

"I don't know," she says, and her teeth are starting to chatter, and the instructor takes a long look at her, and then rubs her shoulders, trying to comfort her, to warm her, and the physical contact feels strange to her, and suddenly she feels overwhelmed by something she doesn't understand, and before she can stop herself, she lunges into the instructor's arms, and sobs and sobs and sobs.

17

TUESDAY

Nate sits next to Genevieve, opposite Detective Casey and Detective Parks.

When Casey had asked if they could ask Genevieve some questions, Rebecca had bristled, but Genevieve had risen obediently. But when Rebecca had moved to stand with her, she'd said, "I want to be with Dad." She'd even moved closer to Nate, almost like she was afraid of her mother, Casey noted, as she waited for one of the parents to speak.

"Of course. Whatever you need, honey." It was Rebecca who spoke, but it was Nate who Gen looked to for confirmation, or reassurance.

Now, Casey waits patiently. She'd asked Genevieve to tell her about Sunday. Genevieve is chewing her lower lip. She glances at Nate anxiously.

"I spent most of it in my room. Mom had had friends over for dinner on Saturday. They're exhausting, Mom's dinners."

"Yeah?" Casey encourages. "How so?"

"Just being social. Being happy. We have to entertain any

kids that come. Beth's daughters were there. Ellie and Minka. They're our ages."

Gen lapses into silence again, and Nate sits beside her, his memories working overtime.

"So do you like them?"

Gen shrugs. "They're fine." She did, in fact, like the girls quite a lot. But it takes so much effort to make friends, to be a good friend. *What's the point?*

"So what happened at dinner?"

Gen gives Nate a sidelong glance, and he braces himself. It's almost apologetic, her look.

"Well, it was the usual stuff. Nice food, the adults were drinking. Tabby and Minka were allowed to have some wine."

Nate stiffens immediately. He and Rebecca had agreed no alcohol before eighteen. It was strict, and hard to enforce, but Nate felt strongly about it. It was bad for their brains, it was bad for their decision-making.

It was bad for teenage girls left alone with handsome stepfathers.

"Mom got a bit drunk. Started being a bit over the top. Leroy was trying to steer the conversation back to safer things but she's like a dog with a bone sometimes. So they were a bit tetchy. Beth and Sandy were both drunk though, I don't think anyone was paying much attention."

But you were, Casey thinks to herself, taking in the serious demeanor, the way Genevieve looked almost like she wanted to protect her father from something.

"What were they talking about that wasn't safe to talk about?" Casey is gentle, though she's more interested in Sunday than Saturday night.

"Dad getting fired. The message." Here Genevieve looks apologetically at Nate again, and his face flushes. "Leroy was trying to get her to stop. I don't think he likes it when Mom talks about Dad, especially if she's...not saying anything nice. I think he was a bit embarrassed."

Casey looks back to Nate, raises an eyebrow in question. "I didn't think you knew about that," he says to Genevieve, his voice faint. She looks back at him sadly. "We hear you guys fighting." She pauses, then adds, almost bitterly, "We know more than you think."

Casey is impatient to move on to what Genevieve saw on Sunday, though. "Is it relevant? Do I need to know about it?"

"No," says Nate firmly. "It's ancient history. It's got nothing to do with anything." He stops though, and wonders if this is strictly true.

He snapped. He was pushed too far.

Has Tabby snapped? Has she been pushed too far?

"So what about Sunday, Genevieve? Do you know where Tabby was, what she was doing?"

"She was in her room. She was probably studying, or drawing. She draws when she's upset."

Nate looks at Genevieve, surprised. This was news to him. He's never seen his eldest daughter draw anything, not since primary school.

"Why would she have been upset, do you think?"

Genevieve looks at Casey impatiently.

"The dinner. Mom badmouthing Dad. She's not used to alcohol. She shouted at Mom in front of the guests. She said it was Mom's fault that Dad got fired. And everyone went kind of quiet and the dinner ended soon after that. And I went to my room, so I don't know what happened. But Mom would have been mad. And she can be really mean to Tabby when she's mad."

Nate and Casey are both staring at Genevieve, and she shifts uncomfortably in the plastic chair.

"Can I have some water?" she says, and Casey nods, and gets up to get her some. But when she returns, Genevieve has clammed up.

"Do you know if your mom went to her, if they fought? Or maybe they fought on Sunday?"

But Gen just shrugs. "I was in my room. I was listening to music. I didn't hear anything." And she turns her face into Nate's shoulder, and they can't draw out another word.

———

NATE TAKES Genevieve out to sit with Rebecca, then goes back to make a statement to Casey by himself.

He feels sick again, his stomach churning with all the things he hasn't allowed himself to think about since he left Rebecca.

Casey doesn't waste any time.

"Why did you and Rebecca split up?"

She notices how Nate stiffens, but he looks her in the eye. "Rebecca...has very high standards about things. She...likes things done her way. She's pretty controlling, to be honest. She has a bad temper. I just...couldn't live like that anymore."

Casey sits up straighter in her chair. "A bad temper with you? With the kids?"

"With me. I could never live up to her standards. It was just exhausting. I just woke up one day and decided to leave."

Casey considers this with interest. She suspects that that is not the whole story, but wants to try to get a timeline for Sunday, and everyone keeps circling back to Saturday night.

"I noticed that Genevieve wanted you to be with her to talk to me, not her mother. Do you think the girls are scared of her?"

"What? No, I don't think so," Nate says, because that's what he's always told himself, and if he says yes, then what sort of father does that make him? But then he remembers Gen not wanting to stay with Rebecca the day before. And he remembers, with a start, Tabby asking to move in with him a couple of months ago. She'd been so offhand about it, like it didn't matter at all, like it was just some little idea she'd had. And yet when he'd said no—*his place was so small!* The girls had to a share a room when they stayed with him. Ever since he lost his job, he's been doing casual work, he can't afford anything bigger—Tabby had collapsed into herself. She'd tried to hide it, and Nate had been uneasy. But he'd asked more questions, and she'd brushed it off as a silly idea, nothing to worry about, and he *knew* he should have pressed more, but the truth was, he didn't really want to ask too many questions about Rebecca and that house.

If he didn't ask questions, he couldn't get answers he didn't like, could he? a biting, scornful, disgusted part of himself pipes up, and Nate cringes in his chair.

"So what days do you usually have the girls?"

"Tuesday and Wednesday. And most of the school holidays. As they've gotten older they've wanted to have more of one base," he adds defensively, wanting to shout that it wasn't *his* idea to have them less.

Except it was his idea, wasn't it? Saturdays were his idea. Tabby was at work all day anyway, and he could pick up some casual work on Saturdays, and it had very much been his idea.

"Why did you get fired?"

Nate sighs in exasperation. "Is this really important right now? Is it going to help you find my daughter?"

"Officers are looking for your daughter," Casey reassures him. "I just want to try to get the whole picture."

"I sent an inappropriate message to someone. It was stupid. She just wrote something stupid on Facebook, commented some stupid thing about men being violent. And I never get into these arguments online. Like, I know they're stupid. I know cowards hide behind their keyboards. I know you should never, never get involved. But that day, I was just so angry. I was so fed up. And I sent her a very awful message, and she took a screenshot of it and sent it to my boss. And I got fired. Okay?"

He had apologized. He had nearly died of shame. He couldn't believe he could be so stupid. He had never done anything like it before or since. It was just that day. At that moment. And even now, as he thinks about it, he can feel the rage rising in his chest, the unfairness of it, the *childishness* of it. That some stupid woman somewhere could make such stupid, blanket statements about men, without even knowing him!

Without knowing what he went through.

Just that morning, the day of the message, he'd been up early, getting the girls ready for school. He'd been in a good mood, humming to himself as he made their sandwiches. He hadn't even resented that Rebecca was still in bed, not helping at all, which was becoming a pattern on school days. He used to think if he just did more, if he supported her more, if he took on more and more responsibility with the kids, then Rebecca would be happier. Less grumpy. Less on edge.

Less vile.

And he'd taken the kids to school, picked them up, taken them to tennis, helped them with their homework, and then, after dinner, he'd said something casual, offhand, about an early meeting he had the next day, and had joked perhaps it was Rebecca's turn to do school drop-off. And of course there was a barb in there. Of course there was. But it was still mostly good-natured. He was mostly just looking for a laugh, an acknowledgement of how much he did, something a little more like how they used to tease each other. Because he really didn't mind doing more, even doing most of the kid stuff. He didn't mind if it made Rebecca happier.

But he should have known better.

There had been no good-natured teasing for quite some time.

The way she had reared back, like a snake about to strike. The *ferociousness* on her face.

The image still chills him.

"You do what I tell you to do with those children or I'll eat them for breakfast," she'd hissed, the rage and hatred palpable, and how could he explain it to people? It wasn't the words, and he didn't really believe she would do anything to hurt their children. It was her loss of control, however fleeting, however quickly she reined it back in. And it was her knowledge, and his knowledge, that he would do whatever she said because she was in charge, and she was terrifying.

Ever since he'd left, he still couldn't explain it to himself, let alone anyone else. Why was he so afraid of her anger? She was never physically violent. But something in her demeanor, her lack of control, her ferocity was utterly chilling. Like maybe he *did* believe she might hurt him? Hurt their children to get back at him? He still couldn't say with any certainty. All he knew was that he scrambled to do her bidding out of a real and genuine fear about what would follow if he did not. But whenever he tried to tell someone, to try to trace out the craziness of it, it sounded so utterly ludicrous that *he* felt ashamed.

Later that night, still in shock, still trying to work out how he had found himself in this position, with a wife who seemed to hate him, who seemed hell-bent on destroying him if he stepped out of her carefully prescribed lines, well he'd just seen this post on Facebook, some woman saying how controlling men were, how they should all be shot for the things they did to women, and he'd felt so powerless, so outraged, because his experience was the exact opposite, wasn't it?

He was not some misogynistic jerk who terrorized his wife.

He was actually a spineless jerk who let himself get terrorized by her.

And he'd hit "message" on her profile and told her he hoped some hero would bend her over a table and fuck her with a kitchen knife, and he didn't even think about it.

He didn't know what he hoped to achieve. He wasn't a violent person and he never, ever thought about hurting people, about causing anyone any pain. And it certainly wasn't a way of convincing that woman that what she said wasn't true. It made absolutely no sense, but do you make sense when your brain is clouded with fear, and confusion, and anger? When everything you thought about how a marriage worked was just not holding up against reality, and all the things you'd usually do as an adult to try to reason, negotiate, work through these problems was met with either gaslighting or more emotionally violent rage?

He just wanted somewhere safe to express his anger. And it wasn't safe at home. And that poor woman, she was just an easy target in that moment, when he didn't know where to put all his feelings, didn't know who he could blame. And while he'd never condone it, he'd never try to defend it, he could think it through carefully enough to understand where it came from and know he would never repeat it. But he could see how he got there. As mortifying and awful as the whole thing was...he could understand it.

Lashing out is what powerless people do.

As he sits there though, all he can think about is the fact that he left his kids in that space, and never asked any questions about whether they were okay.

Of course Rebecca had told everyone that that was why they'd separated, made him out to be the violent, awful one. And that goddamn message, it was so much easier to hold up as a "bad thing" than the subtle things that Rebecca did, that he couldn't properly articulate, that seemed so trite when he tried to explain them.

"Nate?"

Casey watched the emotions flash across Nate's face and her mind is ticking over with all the questions she needs to ask.

Firstly, for someone who claimed his wife had a temper, why he looked so full of rage and anger himself.

But there was something else in there which makes her senses sit on high alert.

Shame.

She knows that shame can instigate all sorts of bad behavior, and she wonders if Nate is ashamed because he acted badly, or if he acted badly because he is ashamed.

"There's something else," Nate says, eager to move away from this topic, to move the spotlight onto other men. Worse men. "I overheard the girls fighting. Gen was telling Tabby that someone was too old for her and it was disgusting. I don't know who they were talking about."

Casey sits up very straight. "Have you asked her?"

"What?"

"Genevieve. Have you asked her who the man is?"

For a second Nate looks confused, then embarrassed. His cheeks flush slightly. "Ah, no. I didn't think to. I mean, we asked if Tabby was seeing anyone. But I didn't bring up what I'd heard."

Casey looks at Nate thoughtfully. She thinks that if a father thought his sixteen-year-old daughter was seeing an older man, he'd be asking questions. *Nate can't seriously expect her to believe he just heard that, and let it go?* She thinks about this for a moment, then tells him as much.

He does, however, look convincingly chagrined.

"The girls... I thought they wouldn't tell me. They're very loyal to each other. I don't want to...disrupt that. I thought I'd just try to...work it out myself." Nate's embarrassment deepens, but he stumbles on, knowing how he sounds: "I thought Tabby might be going to see the guy on Sunday, so I waited outside the house. I know how it sounds. I shouldn't have done it. And now, Christ." Nate rubs his forehead.

"And?" Casey is disbelieving. *What sort of father behaves this way?* She actually can't even answer that question. If Nate was wanting to control his daughter, he would have sat her down and demanded answers, not let her out of his sight. *Was it weakness? It certainly seemed like stupidity. If you had a good relationship, you'd just ask a few questions, right? Try to guide, or at least understand?*

"She came home on her bike about 10 p.m. She was coming from the west. She seemed calm. She didn't see me." He hesitates. He might as well come clean. Hell, he doesn't know what to do with this information. He might as well give it to someone who might be able to make sense of it.

"I thought it might be Leroy, okay? Have you seen pictures? Tabby is stunning. Men look at her wherever she goes. She spends a lot of time with Leroy, Rebecca works a lot, goes away for work a lot. He's a good-looking guy. I thought maybe I'd see him coming home ten minutes later. But I didn't." A pause. "I did see him later, though."

Cringing at what he's admitting to—lurking creepily outside his ex-wife's house for hours—he nevertheless goes on: "Leroy came out at about midnight. He was pacing around, agitated. He was on the phone, or trying to call someone, getting frustrated. He was probably outside for about ten minutes. Then he went back inside and I went home."

18

THREE MONTHS Earlier

Rebecca is lying on Tabby's bed, her eyes squeezed tightly shut.

The girls are both at school, and Rebecca needs to go to work. She's nearly going.

Almost.

The night before keeps playing, over and over, as vivid as if it were happening right now. She doesn't know why she can't shake it. It's not like it's different than any other fight.

They're all much the same, if she was really honest with herself.

Her impulse is to go shopping. Buy something nice for herself, and a few more nice things for Tabby. Designer clothes. Delicate, intricate jewelry that all Tabby's friends would notice, be envious over.

That's what Rebecca usually does when she feels this uneasy swirl of difficult emotions. She just replaces them with better ones.

Is it just because of Moira?

The thought shocks her, slapping into her psyche out of nowhere, jolting her eyes open.

Of course not. It's got nothing to do with Moira.

Tabby was doing it on purpose. After everything Rebecca does for that child. She sends her to a good school, she pays for luxurious family holidays. She gives her free rein in the kitchen to order food and bake whatever she likes. *Is it so much to ask that Tabby show a bit of respect in return?*

What even was it over last night? Tabby had come home late. Rebecca missed the days when they baked cupcakes together, when Tabby would invite all her friends around to cook and watch movies. Rebecca had felt like one of their gang, young and carefree and trendy. She loved being around those girls. She loved posing with them for photos and sharing them on social media. Feeling like a good mother, a connected mother.

A cool mother.

When had they stopped visiting?

She'd just tried to reminisce a little with Tabby. She'd just asked why she didn't invite her friends over anymore, she even suggested she invite them this weekend, and Rebecca would shop for whatever ingredients she liked. They could go wild in the kitchen, she'd said. And Tabby had rolled her eyes at her.

Rebecca had tried, she really had. She'd been gentle, she'd asked if Tabby wanted to talk about why she didn't invite her friends over anymore, so they could all hang out like they used to. "I miss that," Rebecca had said. *She was trying to connect with Tabby, for God's sake.*

And Tabby had stood there, something strange passing across her face, *was that contempt that Rebecca saw?* She had looked undecided, like she was thinking about what to say, for a moment Rebecca thought she even might cry, but then there was that contemptuous look, and what had she said? Rebecca can barely remember through the roar in her ears, the disbelief.

"What? So you can pretend we're one big happy family?" And then, the anger seeping out of her and turning into something else: "I don't invite them because I'm afraid you'll lose your temper in front of them." Whispered, eyes wide. And it was ludicrous, people *loved* Rebecca, they always wanted to sit with her, to share an office, to be invited to her house, it was *insulting,* like Tabby had somehow lost her friends but wanted to blame Rebecca, make it her fault that they never visited anymore, and honestly it was hard to think about, because she just felt furious. And Tabby had said she'd be home at ten and it was at least half past, and she'd just lost it a little bit, screamed a few things, snatched Tabby's phone out of her hands, confiscated it for a week.

And Tabby had *smirked.*

That was different, that wasn't how things usually went. Usually, Rebecca would lose her temper, and she'd feel bad, and maybe she'd buy Tabby something nice to show her that there were no hard feelings, that she was forgiven. She *wants* to be a good mom, she thinks about how to be a good mom. It's just. Well. She doesn't know why she gets so angry It's inexplicable. It's like a tsunami of rage comes up out of nowhere, rushes through her and out of her and crashes into Tabby. It's always been like this, and then it's over, as quickly as it started and she wishes she hadn't yelled, and she can't quite remember what it was she said, but if only Tabby could just be honest about her problems, why her friends don't visit, if only she didn't make it Rebecca's fault, *why was she like this?*

But today, for the first time, something uneasy churns inside Rebecca.

They always make up, it's always fine.

But that look last night.

Rebecca burrows into Tabby's pillow. She can't quite put her finger on what it is that's wrong. Partly, it's the uneasy sense that she's lost control of something. That Tabby, who usually cowers and flees, who tries to make it up to Rebecca, who tries so hard to be good for weeks after a fight—*everything is so calm and peaceful, for a little while*—last night just looked completely untouched by it. Completely indifferent. For a moment, she looked like she always looked—fragile and sorry—but then there was that smirk, like she didn't care that Rebecca took her phone, that she didn't care that Rebecca was angry with her. It feels like something slipping through her fingers, something that seemed predictable and certain and, God, it was just the dance they did, wasn't it? Their mother daughter dance. Tabby trying to push boundaries and Rebecca holding the fort.

Why does it feel different, this time, though?

"I'm afraid you'll lose your temper in front of them."

What did that even mean? Was her yelling worse than other mothers'? She had never yelled in front of Tabby's friends, what was Tabby even talking about?

Rebecca feels the familiar rage bubbling in her chest. And half of her wants to burrow into Tabby's pillow and cry, but she doesn't understand the feeling, and she pushes it away angrily, and lumbers out of bed to get ready for work, plastering a bright smile on her face, and thinking there will be no jewelry for that bloody child, she's sick of feeling guilty about yelling at her when frankly, she's such an ungrateful little shit.

19

Rebecca wakes with a start.

She lies in bed, very still.

What had woken her?

Rustling. She strains to hear in the dark, her heart thumping in her chest. For the third or fourth time that day, she's grateful Nate is sleeping down the hallway. If he wasn't here, being woken by strange noises in the night would be terrifying.

There's nothing. Her heart keeps pounding though, as though it knows something she doesn't. She takes some deep slow breaths.

Leroy.

The bed is empty beside her. She feels it acutely, like a cold, icy lump where his warm body should be. It still doesn't feel real. Here, in the dark, her heart hammering in her ears, it can't possibly be more than a bad dream, can it?

She gets out of bed and pads down the hallway to the kitchen. She can see the green glow of the clock and squints to make out the time.

1:01 a.m.

She's just thinking she'll make a cup of tea when she notices a slash of light underneath the door of Tabby's bedroom, and stops in her tracks.

Tabby?

Her instinct is to throw the door open, see her daughter there, crush her to her chest, look after her and love her and cherish her, but she stops herself.

Rustling. She remembers what woke her, and strains to hear if there's any rustling now.

Nate's door is shut, but he's right there. *Should she wake him?*

Instead she shakes herself. If someone was in Tabby's room, it is most likely Tabby, and whatever is going on, Tabby is the only one who can explain it. So she steps forward confidently and flings open the door.

And shivers.

The window is wide open, and the room is freezing.

The orderliness that Rebecca had admired only a couple of days ago is now thrust into disarray: pens scattered across the desk, doonas thrown on the floor. The trundle mattress is half out of its trundle, gently sighing onto the floor, its sheets rumpled and messy.

Someone has been searching for something. Springing into action, she sprints to the window, her eyes searching the parts of their yard she can see. "NATE!" she yells toward his door, and she runs past to the front door, flinging it open, dashing from one end of the veranda to the other, a useless activity— she can't see anything in the dim light.

Further down the road, a streetlamp throws a cool light onto the road and frontyards, but in front of her house, it's dark and silent.

Nate appearing beside her makes her jump.

"Bec?" he says, rubbing his eyes, looking confused and middle-aged in the cheap pyjamas she'd loaned to him; a gift for Leroy from some relative with no sense of taste. Pyjamas she wouldn't let Leroy wear in a pink fit. "What's going on?"

"Someone was in Tabby's room," she says, breathless, marching back into the house and surveying the mess again. "The light. The window."

"The mess," Nate adds, fully awake now. "What were they searching for? Jesus."

"Don't touch anything," Rebecca snaps when Nate steps into the room. "I'll call the police."

AFTER THE OFFICERS HAVE GONE, Nate and Rebecca sit at the kitchen table.

The police had dusted for fingerprints, though Rebecca had had to push for it—she couldn't say if anything was missing, and had to press them that Tabby was missing and Leroy was dead, so they were dealing with a possible homicide investigation, not a case of a missing iPhone. When she said this, she stopped abruptly, thinking of Tabby's second phone. They hadn't managed to locate it, didn't even know its number.

The police had suggested Rebecca check and fasten all the locks.

Now, they sit in silence.

Genevieve has not stirred—or at least, she hasn't emerged, if she heard anything.

"Let her sleep," Nate had said, his hand on Rebecca's arm as she headed for Genevieve's door, and she'd stopped, looked down at his hand pointedly. Nate had removed it.

"She needs to tell us who Tabby's lover is."

Rebecca had wasted no time asking her after they left the police station the day before, but Genevieve had looked alarmed, and denied she knew anything. When Rebecca had recounted what Nate had overheard, Gen got a stubborn look on her face, and insisted they were talking about celebrity crushes.

"Oh, come on, Gen." Rebecca had been angry. "You don't get angry about celebrity crushes. 'Mind your own fucking business'?" But Genevieve was sticking to her story and remained stony-faced.

Minutes tick by. Nate rubs his face. He's doing it repeatedly, like he's trying to rub away this reality, and the gesture irks Rebecca. "Maybe I misheard," he says now. "Maybe she's telling the truth." *Maybe I was primed to hear things that implicate Leroy in something seedy,* he admits to himself, but not to Rebecca.

"Why don't you go back to bed, try to get some rest," he says, gentle. "You've had a terrible shock. I can't imagine what you're going through. I'll sit up and keep an eye on things."

The thought of a stranger in the house, with Genevieve asleep in the bedroom next door, makes his heart thud in his chest. They had peeked in, of course, to check that Gen was all right, that she hadn't been disturbed (*or taken,* Nate realizes), but she'd looked peaceful, her dark hair fanned across her pillow, her mouth slightly open.

He'd clicked the door shut ever so gently, even though he knows she could sleep through an avalanche.

Rebecca shakes her head at him. "I'll never get back to sleep," she says, and he nods.

He puts his head in his hands and squeezes his eyes shut.

Eventually he looks up.

"Tell me about the fight," he says, and his eyes brook no resistance.

I know, and you know, they seem to be saying to her.

But now we need to talk about it.

Rebecca looks uncertain.

"It was nothing," she says, defensive. "She was being disrespectful. I told you. I yelled at her, told her not to be so disrespectful. After all the things I do for her. Yada yada yada."

Her face clouds over, and Nate can see indecision, anger, and even self-doubt passing across it with her thoughts, but she won't be drawn on anymore.

"Our daughter is missing!" he shouts in frustration. "Don't you think it might be relevant? You and I both know your fights can get completely out of hand. *What did you say to her?*"

But Rebecca just put her head in her hands, and refused to say another word.

Alone in her bed later, she turns Nate's words over and over in mind.

Did she know?

There's that creeping feeling in her stomach, the uneasiness she can't shake. The unsettling idea that what she brushed over and smoothed away was not nothing. That there was something about her fights with Tabby that were furtive and shameful. Something that was outside her control, that she couldn't whip back into shape, into something calm and understandable, something justified.

"I'm afraid you'll lose your temper in front of them."

Tabby's words hang in her mind, suspended. They didn't make any sense. Rebecca never lost her temper in front of other people. *Why would Tabby think such a thing?* It was only Tabby who drove her so crazy, who made her so mad. But even as she thinks this, something bubbles and whirs away deep inside her: the knowledge that perhaps that was a problem. *That if she could control her temper in other contexts, why couldn't she control it with Tabby?*

If she could control it when Tabby had a friend over, and wait until the friend had gone to let loose her rage, that if she didn't do it with other people, was it because she knew that it really wasn't an okay way to treat other people? That that flash of satisfaction she feels when she sees Tabby cowering, succumbing, soothes something in her, makes the world feel right again, but she would never, ever,

ever admit that to anyone or resolve a dispute that way outside her home?

That she would never, ever, ever settle some disrespect at work this way?

In amongst all these questions though, another one pops up, and it is the question that lingers on her mind, and scares and confuses her the most. She shoves it away, trying desperately to go to sleep, but it keeps resurfacing, taunting her, scaring her.

That word. The last thing that Leroy ever said to her.

Abuse.

Angrily, she leaps out of bed and pops a sleeping tablet from the pack, swallowing it in a fury.

But the question doesn't leave her. In amongst the drugged heaviness that starts to wash over her, in fact, it's the one phrase that remains crystal clear.

If her "abuse" is a problem...can she stop?

20

Two-and-a-Half Months Earlier

"What's wrong, Freddy?"

Rebecca stops what she is doing in surprise when Freddy comes into the kitchen. She's wiping away tears, but she looks angry, too.

"Honey, are you okay? Did you and Tabby have a fight?" Rebecca pats a barstool and sits down herself, but Freddy stays standing, her posture stiff. Like she doesn't know whether to trust Rebecca or view her as the enemy.

"Here, come try this for me," Rebecca goes on, scooping some icing out of her mixmaster. It's streaked red and white and is rich and buttery. Rebecca already knows it's good, she doesn't need Freddy to tell her, but she proffers the spoon anyway. Hoping to tip Freddy's assessment from suspicious to trusting. She's never seen Freddy and Tabby fight before.

Freddy hesitates for a moment, then obediently steps closer and opens her mouth.

"Oh gosh, so good, Mrs. G. What's it for?"

"I just felt like baking. It's nice to have treats in the kitchen, don't you think?" Rebecca doesn't look at Freddy, but busies herself scraping the icing onto a fat pale cake on a fancy cake stand. She scrapes and smooths and spreads with flourishes. Within minutes, the cake looks like something you might buy in a shop.

Freddy sits herself down on the edge of the barstool gingerly. She seems deep in thought.

"You can take some home if you like," Rebecca offers, indicating the cake.

"Oh no, that's okay," Freddy says, looking uncomfortable. She doesn't want to put Rebecca out, but she also doesn't want to carry half a cake home on her bike.

"Well, the offer's there. Or you can just sneak a piece now if you prefer."

Freddy nods at this. "Seems a shame to cut into it, though, doesn't it?"

"Not at all. It will be demolished by dinnertime. You've seen this family eat!" Rebecca smiles at Freddy, trying to draw her out of herself. She looks so forlorn. "You look like you need a hug, sweetie," she goes on, opening her arms, and Freddy looks surprised. But she moves toward Rebecca, and then it's Rebecca's turn to be surprised, because Freddy bursts into tears.

Rebecca strokes her back gently. "You want to talk about it?"

Freddy looks down. She loves Tabby, she really does, but it's hard to love her at the moment, and it's hard to reconcile the things Tabby says about Rebecca with the woman Freddy always sees when she comes over: warm, humorous, teasing. And of course she's on Tabby's side, she'll always be on Tabby's side, but Rebecca is always so nice to her, so funny, so generous. And Tabby has just been so...corrosive recently. Picking fights, moody, all friendly and smiling one moment and asking Freddy to leave the next. It's hard to keep up with her mood swings. And if she's very honest with herself, Freddy might even say that it would serve Tabby right for Freddy to tell Rebecca what's going on.

"She's just so moody at the moment," Freddy says, and despite her anger, another tear escapes, slides down her cheek. "I know she's having a hard time. I try to be a good friend. But she just snapped at me. It's like she doesn't even want me here. And she says it's about you, Mrs. G." Here Freddy looks apologetic. "But I know that's not the reason. I know there's something else going on."

Rebecca doesn't look up. She carefully cuts a couple of thick slices of cake. "About me? Huh. What does she say about that?" Her voice is carefully light, perplexed. Freddy looks guilty, but Rebecca pushes the cake toward her, smiling. "We have had a few fights recently. Just normal teenage stuff, though. You fight with your mom, right?"

"Yeah." Freddy grins. "All the time. She's always on my back about schoolwork and getting off the phone." She takes a bite and closes her eyes. "God, this is good, Mrs. G. You could open a shop."

"It's just the same with Tabby, right?" Rebecca pushes, careful, eyes on the cake.

"Yeah. She just says you're always shouting at her. She's gotten really sensitive lately. I just asked if I could stay the night. She hasn't wanted me to for months. I miss sleeping here, hanging out more." Freddy scrunches her face up, holding back tears. "I went to pull the trundle out and she just shouted at me that she didn't want me here, told me to leave. I don't think she even wants to be my friend anymore." Freddy looks sadly at her cake. "And I don't know what it is I've done wrong."

That's not entirely true, though. Freddy does have an inkling. There was that dinner party here a couple of months ago, and Mrs. G had let them both have a glass of wine, which she does sometimes, and Freddy had felt so happy. She and

Tabby had laughed so much. Tabby had seemed carefree, delighted by life, laughing at everything Freddy had to say. They'd been lying on Tabby's bed, talking rubbish, both a little bit drunk—neither were used to wine, and it went straight to their heads.

Rebecca's friends had left, and the house had grown quiet. And the wine had made her brave. Lying in Tabby's single bed, their limbs entwined, their heads close together to talk and share Tabby's phone, it had felt so right. So natural. And of course Freddy had thought about it before—many, many times before—but in that moment, she didn't think about it. Maybe because it was on her mind so much it was almost like they were a couple already, and she'd just run a hand up Tabby's thigh to her waist, her fingers light, like it was almost nothing, like she could deny it ever happened if need be. Turning toward her, slipping one leg between Tabby's, she'd breathed, "I want to stay the night." And Tabby had sat up abruptly, the moment catapulted from sensual to something else entirely, not meeting Freddy's eye.

"I've got some studying to do," she'd said, though they both knew that was untrue—it was nearly 11 p.m. and Tabby was tipsy. "You should probably go home."

Neither of them had ever mentioned it since, not even hinted at it, and Freddy was mortified. Mortified that she'd misread Tabby's affection; mortified that she'd been rejected. Mortified that their friendship had waned ever since and she'd ruined it, ruined everything.

She was also a little bit angry, because Tabby could have just pretended it never happened. She didn't need to make it so obvious, did she? Sitting up so violently. Removing Freddy from the room, from her house. *Like, she could have made it easier for Freddy, couldn't she?* She could have let her save face.

But mostly she was devastated because she wanted to kiss

Tabby so badly, and apparently Tabby did not have any desire whatsoever to kiss her back.

Rebecca watches this conflict pass across Freddy's face, and wonders what it is that's happened between them. "She's become pretty quiet recently with everyone, honey," she says now, kindly. "I'm sure it's not just you. I think she's studying hard and is just going through a moody phase. Do you want me to talk to her?"

Freddy looks alarmed. "God no, please don't say anything." She thinks that if Tabby's mad at her now, knowing she'd spoken candidly to Rebecca would make it a thousand times worse. Though for the life of her, she can't work out why Tabby has so much hostility toward her mother. Rebecca seems to spoil Tabby rotten. Freddy wished her mother would buy her designer clothes and custom jewelry. "I'm sure it will be fine tomorrow. She just needs a bit more space than she used to. And I still want things to be the same as they always were."

Not quite the same though, Freddy thinks to herself. The sleepovers, the easy camaraderie, the mucking around.

But maybe also a bit of kissing and touching each other, too.

21

WEDNESDAY

Loud knocking on the door drags Nate from his dreams.

Shit.

He was meant to be looking out for them all, not sleeping on the kitchen table.

Opening the door, it takes him a moment to recognize the couple standing on the doorstep.

"*Nate?*" Cheryl squints at him, like she can't quite believe her eyes.

Nate just stares back, equally perplexed.

He hasn't seen Rebecca's parents in at least ten years. He's only met them a handful of times. They didn't even come to his and Rebecca's wedding.

For a moment, he fumbles over their names. "Cheryl. Rob. Hi."

They all stand around awkwardly, then Nate shakes himself, and invites them inside.

"Coffee?" he asks, thinking that unless things have changed remarkably since he left, Rebecca is going to wake up and lose her mind.

Not his problem anymore.

A few hours earlier, she had eventually agreed to go back to bed. Nate glances at the clock. 8:01 a.m. At least they both got a little sleep, even if he failed in his protective duties.

He supposes letting Cheryl and Rob into the house might be considered a double failure.

"No, thanks. We had some on the way." There's a long pause, then Cheryl adds, "Rebecca's not returning our calls. Genevieve filled us in."

Nate looks up sharply. He didn't even know Genevieve knew her grandparents' phone number, let alone would call them in a time of distress.

"It's nice to see you, Nate." Cheryl looks emotional, and for a moment Nate thinks she is going to burst into tears. Her husband puts his hand over hers.

Nate busies himself making a coffee for himself. The very idea of emotional ex-parents-in-law in his ex-wife's kitchen is making his head hurt. If he's honest, he can't even remember any of the details why Rebecca didn't talk to her parents. *They had a falling out? They were uninvolved when she was a kid, and she was happy to leave home and leave them behind?* Rebecca certainly never filled him in, and did not welcome any inquiries on the matter. All he can remember her saying was "we're just not a close family, okay?"

He wishes he'd shown more interest. It suited him to not delve into that. It seemed difficult, and fraught, and he'd just let it slide.

"It's been a long time," Nate says now, slowly. "The kids must have been tiny. One of their birthdays, maybe?"

"No. We were never invited to their birthdays." Cheryl holds Nate's eyes steadily. "We dropped in on Moira's birthday one year. Tabby was six."

Nate remembers the day with a start. Rebecca had been

furious, had sent them packing. Never mind that they'd driven three hours to see her.

"It's just like them to not give me notice, just expect me to drop everything," she had fumed. She had a hair appointment and she refused to postpone it; *her hairdresser was so hard to get in to, she wouldn't get another chance for months.*

Nate had had the feeling that she was glad of the excuse.

"I didn't realize it was Moira's birthday," Nate says now, perplexed that that was the day that they had chosen to visit. "You must still miss her." *Did they try to visit Rebecca because they wanted to be with family on Moira's birthday? To reminisce? To support each other?* He pauses, and no one fills the silence. "I'm sorry you couldn't stay that day. I don't really understand your relationship with Rebecca. She never wanted to talk about it." He feels guilty still, as though he ought to be giving them the cold shoulder, showing his allegiance to Rebecca, even though she refused to share the details of why. He can't shake the need to be a good husband.

A good ex-husband.

"Yes, well." Cheryl looks primly down at the table. "You and us both. But now's not the time to quibble over past differences, is it? We want to help. Tell us what we can do."

"Well. The police are looking for Tabby. But someone was in her room last night. Looking for something. So perhaps—"

"*What?*" Rob is on his feet. He's a big man.

"We thought she'd run away?"

"Look, we don't know what happened. But someone needs to be with Gen. That's probably the best you can do to help. Take her out of here, even. If she'll go, and if Rebecca agrees to it."

"Agrees to what?"

Rebecca is standing in the doorway, slowly taking in the scene in her kitchen. She looks tired. Nate realizes he's holding his breath. He lets it out with a long sigh.

"Something bothering you, Nate?" Rebecca fixes him with a steely stare, and Nate has to remind himself that this is not his family anymore.

It's not his problem.

Well, that's not quite true, is it? he thinks to himself. *They're always going to be family, whether he likes it or not. But he doesn't have to fix this. He doesn't have to solve it, or save anyone.*

"Hello, Mom. Hello, Dad." Rebecca turns to her parents, her voice cool. "Still not big on giving notice, I see." She looks determined to be frosty, but Nate thinks she also looks as though she might cry. He feels completely clueless about their family dynamics.

"I was just telling your folks we think someone broke into Tabby's room last night. That perhaps it might be good for Gen to not be here for a while. Gen filled them in on what's been going on here. Honestly, I don't know what they can help with. What do you think?"

"It might be a good idea. Sure." Nate nearly falls over in surprise. *Rebecca trusts them with Genevieve?*

"I won't go." Genevieve peers out from behind Rebecca. Nate didn't hear her get up and wonders how long she has been standing within earshot. Despite her statement, she pushes past Rebecca and runs over to her grandmother and wraps her in a fierce hug.

"Sweetie." Cheryl really does cry now, big fat tears sliding down her cheeks, gasping breaths that she tries to hide. "It's so good to hug you." Rob squeezes Gen's shoulder too, his voice gruff: "Hey, kid."

Nate looks from them to Gen to Rebecca in confusion. Gen has obviously been in touch with her grandparents more than just this incident. And Rebecca is pretending it's all perfectly normal, pulling containers out of the pantry for breakfast.

He wants to shout, "What the hell's going on?" Everything seems to be operating on two levels—the fake, false, shiny upper level where no one says what they mean, and they all just pretend this is a normal family get together; and a murky undertow, where nothing is as it seems.

Why are Cheryl and Rob here?

What has Genevieve told them?

Why is Rebecca letting them stay after decades of refusing to talk about them?

His head is pounding again. All this, on top of—*where the hell is Tabby?*

He can't even think about Leroy.

He just wants his daughter back. Once she's back, he can sort everything else out.

Like how Leroy died, for example.

Like why Tabby wanted to move in with him.

Like if an older man was taking advantage of her.

And how it all related to, oh God—why oh why had he left it this long—the fact that his children were scared of their bloody mother?

22

THE LITTLE GIRL strokes her sister's hair, murmuring soothing, shushing noises.

Her sister is sick, and she is looking after her.

She's stripped her bed and put everything in the wash, and wiped up the vomit as best she can from the carpet. Later, she'll ask her mother how best to remove the stain, and be shouted at because she left it so long, rather than praised for cleaning it up at all.

She doesn't know that yet though.

She's tucked her sister up in her own bed, wiping her brow with a damp face washer.

Her sister is hot. Very hot. But the little girl knows better than to disturb her mother's sleep.

Outside, she can see stars stabbing holes in the sky. As she shushes and murmurs, she wonders what other children are doing. Sleeping, of course. But are they doing better than her? Are they looking after their siblings? Are they getting things right?

Just yesterday, she'd carefully chosen her clothes, brushed her long hair, looked at herself in the mirror and been pleased. She looked pretty, like the girls in the magazines some of the other girls brought to school. For some reason she thought that that was important, that that would please her parents, and now she doesn't know why.

Why had she thought wasting time on her appearance would be a good idea?

Her father had stared at her, his lip curling, and she knew immediately it had been a bad idea.

"You look like a slut, just like your mother," he had said, and her mother had turned on her in a rage. So her father was mad at her and her mother, and it was all her fault.

Except, it was just last week that her father had looked her up and down after school in disgust. "Brush your hair and wear clean clothes to school. You look like a tramp." And she'd worked out how to use the washing machine all by herself. She'd made sure her clothes were clean every day since.

She didn't have a hairbrush, but she had found her mother's in the bathroom, and brushed her locks until they felt silky. She'd brushed her sister's, too.

She was so proud of working out the washing machine.

Now, she strokes her sister's head and watches her sleep. She's restless. She's vomited twice already. The second time the little girl was ready though—she had found a bucket in the laundry, and caught every last drop.

She kisses her sister's brow gently, and can smell the vomit. So she goes and dips the face washer in soapy water from the bathroom, squeezes it out, and gently runs it along the offending hairs, alternately cleaning and cooling her sister.

She loves her sister more than anything in the world.

She would look after her all day, all week, all year if need be.

She watches her little face, and wants to protect her, and make the world better for her sister than it is for her.

23

WEDNESDAY

Watch your back.

The text message pops up on Rebecca's phone and cuts through the awkward silence in Rebecca's kitchen.

Nate has already called Detective Casey, called Freddy again, unable to sit still and wait.

He can't think of anywhere else Tabby might go. Except to her older lover's house, but they have no idea who that might be—except Leroy, however much Rebecca might deny it. *Is there some special place they'd go to meet?*

A dead Leroy supports that theory, in Nate's book. They drive somewhere to... God, he can't even think about it. It makes him want to be sick.

They fought.

Tabby...pushed him off the bridge?

Even to Nate, it sounds far-fetched. Tabby is so slight. Leroy is a well-built guy. He just can't see it playing out that way.

Nothing unusual was found in Leroy's car. Long, blonde hairs, which could be Rebecca's or Tabby's, but they know Tabby has been in the car. There's no point even testing them.

Was she in there on Sunday night is the question.

But there were no signs of a struggle, no body fluids, no unusual objects. The keys were in the ignition, which suggests that Leroy exited the car in a hurry.

Was he chasing someone?

Was he being chased?

Now, they all stare at the phone in stunned silence. It's lying face up; there's no hiding it. It's been seen by everyone sitting around the table.

Thank God Genevieve was in the bathroom.

"It's the same number." Nate is matter-of-fact, reaching for the phone, handing it to Rebecca.

They'd given it to the police, of course, but they were unable to trace it.

Cheryl looks so shocked that Nate feels sorry for her. He explains about the other message. "I should let Detective Casey know." He stands up heavily and goes into the next room, leaving Rebecca alone with her parents.

"What's the link?" Casey muses on the phone to him. "The one to Tabby sounded like someone angry about who she's seeing. A jealous ex. A jilted wife. But the one to Rebecca... Are they threatening Rebecca because they hold her responsible for her daughter's actions?"

Nate starts. "Is she in danger? Are they saying...Leroy was first. You're next?" His heart is hammering wildly in his chest. Rebecca was difficult to live with, but the thought of anyone harming her fills him with terror. "Or are they telling her her husband is having an affair? Are they warning her or threatening her?"

"It would be good if someone stayed with her. Or even if she went to stay in a hotel while we look into this." Casey sounds calm, soothing even, but Nate doubts she makes those kinds of recommendations lightly.

"Her parents are here." Nate hesitates. "They've been

basically estranged for as long as I've known Rebecca. Apparently Genevieve called them and filled them in. She's kept in touch over the years, apparently. We had no idea." He notes that he and Rebecca have become a "we" again overnight, and he shudders, though he can't quite say why. *Is it because it took him so long to untangle himself from that relationship that the thought of getting sucked back into it is terrifying? Because he lost so much of himself in it that he ended up some place where he didn't even recognize himself?*

Is it just a vague sense of danger, being close to this woman?

"Have they said why they're there?"

"They said they want to help. They seem upset. Genuine. Maybe a crisis is an opportunity to reconnect, to reach out?"

"Maybe." Casey sounds thoughtful. "Where are they staying? I might have a chat with them. I'm going to talk to Leroy's parents today too."

Nate startles again. *Leroy's parents.* He forgot that Leroy existed outside of Rebecca, of Tabby. That there would be other people who loved him. People who would be devastated by the loss of him.

He shivers. All he's been able to think is that Leroy was abusing his daughter, and feel relief that he was out of the picture. Now, that realization makes him feel guilty. All he's thought about are his family, not Leroy's.

What if Leroy is innocent?

Nate realizes with a start that it's *his* family that harbor secrets. Maybe Leroy just got caught up in the mess that was the rest of them?

"I'll find out where they're staying. I'll let you know."

Nate returns to the kitchen slowly. "The police might want to talk to you," he tells Cheryl and Rob, and for a second he could swear he sees panic on Rebecca's face, but it's gone as fast as it appeared, and he rubs his eyes. Everything feels too surreal to trust himself.

"We've booked into the Hyatt. We've booked an extra room if Gen wants to stay with Cheryl, and I'll bunk next door." Rob looks at Nate steadily. Nate can't read his expression at all.

"Bec?" Nate still defers to her. He resents it, but he can't help it. "What do you think? Casey thinks perhaps you should stay in a hotel, too."

"Rubbish. What do they think, they've gotten Leroy, now they're coming for me? I'll stay here, in case Tabby comes home." She looks uncertain, though, and Nate wonders if she wants him to stay there, too.

"Do you want me to stay here? And what about Gen, what do you think? She said she won't go."

Genevieve walks back into the room then.

She looks like she's been crying.

"It's all right. I'll go." And she falls into Nate's arms, and is quiet and still.

***

"WHAT DATE?"

Alone in the house, Rebecca is stumped by the question.

They're past the condolences, the pleasantries. Now they're getting into the nitty gritty of what Rebecca wants for the funeral, and she realizes she doesn't even know if Leroy's body has been released by the police.

Flowers and caskets don't seem real; these are choices other wives have to make. Children, for their parents. Not her. Not for Leroy.

She's glad everyone is gone. Nate has gone to ask Freddy some more questions, see if he can find out anything else that could help them to find Tabby. Gen has gone to the Hyatt with Rebecca's parents. The silence engulfs her, soothes her somehow.

"I might have to get back to you," she tells the funeral director faintly, feeling suddenly light-headed.

Are you expected to be competent arranging all these details for your husband's funeral? At any time? Let alone when your daughter is missing? When your parents, who you've avoided for twenty-five years, pop up in your kitchen?

She hangs up the phone, and sits at the table, staring vacantly out the window.

The fridge hums in the background. A magpie warbles across the road. For the first time all spring, it feels like summer is coming. It feels like Rebecca could be in a parallel world, one where Leroy will be home soon, and they'll pour gin and tonics and sit on the deck, a light breeze ruffling their newly donned summer shirts, the endless possibilities of life spread before them, magnificent.

Taken for granted.

It feels so real that Rebecca lets herself lean into it. Her eyes closed, she imagines the crispness of her drink. Leroy urging her to get changed for tennis, her pressing for them to skip it, to have another gin.

Teasing him when she finally acquiesces, lifting her shirt over her head as she walks to the bedroom to find her gym gear, glancing over her shoulder at him coyly. Knowing if she wants, she can derail his tennis plans completely.

A strange sound startles her and her eyes fly open, then she realizes that the noise came from her—a peculiar, low-pitched noise, somewhere between crying and growling, as though she could threaten the longing inside her away, or frighten her unhelpful daydreams back to where they came from—a useless, magical place that she will never get back to, ever again.

How do you plan a funeral, ever?

How does one move past the disbelief, the pain, the emptiness, to organize and think and wrangle something so huge into something that requires so much...planning? So much attention to details?

It doesn't seem possible, and yet that must be how every funeral goes, mustn't it? People left behind in utter chaos, trying to make decisions and get things done?

Rebecca slowly lowers her head to the table, until her forehead is resting against its cool surface. She closes her eyes again. In another life, organizing a funeral would be effortless. It's the sort of thing she should excel at. Order, purpose, ticking things off in a linear fashion.

When will the body be released?

Date, time, casket.

Invitations.

Today, even the first of these steps seems too hard.

She wonders how Genevieve is coping. *Does Gen really keep in touch with Cheryl and Rob?* Something about another parallel world, where her daughter chats to her parents—*about what?*—makes this current reality seem even more untethered.

Do her parents know how to comfort a grieving child? she wonders, and the thought really does untether her, and she stands up and bites down hard on her fist, and screams and screams and screams.

24

Two Months Earlier

Tabby is super careful writing anything down.

She doesn't share anything that could be identifying. But sometimes she just needs to write her thoughts out, trying to work them out. She always feels better at the end of a writing session.

She hates the word *diary*. Diary sounds like something a nine-year-old would keep. Whining and bitching. She thinks what she does is something far superior to that.

Now, she writes: *I think he really loves me. I think I can finally leave this shithole and be free. We made love today in his bed, and it was kind of gross being in* her *bed, and I did feel kind of guilty, because separation is hard for kids, we should know, and I feel bad about that, God.*

Poor Gen.

So...her bed. So weird. But she never wants to make love to him anymore, he told me it's been years, which is so surprising, because they've always been so touchy, for as long as I can remember, but I suppose they maybe just love each other like friends, not lovers.

Lovers.

Her stomach flip flops all over the place when she thinks about his tongue on her nipples, the way he stares into her eyes as he touches her, like he wants to know all of her, inside and out. She's never felt so seen, so known.

She thinks she could tell him anything.

I had another fight with Mom, she writes. I think I'm starting to work it out. It's not just that she has a temper. It's when I stand up to her. Or when she feels rejected. I can see it come across her face. It's fury, yes, but it's also first this tiny flicker of something else. Desperation? Panic? It's like she feels something bad, and so she has to make me feel worse, and that makes her bad feelings go away. I used to think it was me, that I did something wrong, I'd try so hard to fix it. I'd cry at her feet, literally, like she winded me, like I couldn't breathe, because it was so unexpected, so out of the blue, it was bewildering, her words were always so violent, so painful. And I'd tiptoe around her for weeks, terrified of it happening again, never knowing when it would come out of nowhere and knock me out.

But now I think I know the pattern. I've even tested it a bit. Seen her getting agitated, and said exactly the thing that I think will tip her over the edge, and it's worked every time.

Leroy has a heart attack, poor soul. He can see what I'm doing, even if my mother can't.

But because I can see it coming, it doesn't knock the wind out of me. It's almost funny. I feel like I'm in control now. It's always been her, controlling me, and I've jumped through every damn hoop she's held up to me, like a stupid little lapdog. Jump, jump, jump. When I think about it now, it seems crazy. It's not like she ever hit me. What was I so afraid of?

Well, it's me holding the hoops up now. I've finally grown up. I've found someone who loves me, who doesn't try to control me, and we're going to be together. He just has to tie up a few loose ends. The way he looks at me makes my insides go crazy. I'll never get tired of kissing him. And he worships me. The way he touches me. Ohhhhh. It makes Trent stupid Witherall seem like a robot. I never dreamed I could be this happy. And I feel bad about...well. It doesn't matter. It's worth it for this kind of love. I can leave here. I can make my own decisions.

She thinks back to the first time they were together.

The tenth of June.

She'd been upset about another fight. It was so hard to explain to people. All they see is this successful, charming, empathic woman. They see her showering Tabby with love and gifts. And she tries to say—*it's after a fight. She buys me things after a fight.* And they ask what they fight about, and Tabby feels so stupid and small. Like that time Freddy came over and Tabby took her straight to her room, and didn't stop to say hello to Rebecca. And Rebecca had popped her head in later, and said, "I didn't know Freddy was here, Tabby. Why are you keeping her all to yourself, not sharing her with the rest of us?" And it had been so jokey. Joke, joke, joke. But Tabby could hear the edge in her voice. And she'd smiled uneasily, thinking, *she won't yell with Freddy here.* Because she never yelled in front of other people. Not even Leroy.

Leroy had never seen Rebecca out of control.

He'd seen Tabby's distress. But it was always after the event, not during.

Later, when Freddy had gone home and Tabby was cleaning her teeth, her mother had stopped at the bathroom door, her eyes on Tabby, something flashing across her face, and Tabby braced herself, because she already knew what was coming. She could feel it underneath the jokes.

Earlier, Freddy had glowed a little bit, because everyone loved being noticed by Rebecca. Everyone loved the feel of her affection and admiration falling on them. Even Tabby still glowed when that warmth was directed at her. No matter how much she knew, no matter how many times it happened, she still fell for it every time Rebecca extended her love. *Like this time it might really be better.*

This time it might last.

She yearned toward Rebecca like a stupid moth to a stupid light.

It was never better, though. When Rebecca loved her, she leaned into it, giddy with relief. And then it was withdrawn, and the violence of it took her breath away. Shocked her, every time.

Idiot.

That night, cleaning her teeth, she was beginning to turn a corner, beginning to realize it was a cycle and it was never going to change.

But she could leave.

She could leave, with him.

And it would all be better.

Rebecca's words had hurt her a little less, for the first time. But what she did remember was how no one understood. No one believed her. She had tried to tell Freddy about it: "She was mad I didn't share you with her the other night. She came into the bathroom, and I could see the rage on her face. And it only settles after she's been cruel."

Freddy had looked shocked. "What did she do?"

"She said 'Freddy comes to me when you two fight, you know. She knows you're the one with the shitty temper, not me. We sit and have cake and talk about how mean you can be.'"

Freddy had looked embarrassed, and dubious. "Once. I was upset and spoke to her once, after—" She doesn't finish the sentence. She does think that was a shitty thing of Mrs. G to tell Tabby, but her thoughts are clouded by her own sense of betrayal about the context of that conversation. "Well, that is a shitty thing to say to you. But it doesn't sound like something worth getting upset over, does it? She was sad that you two were fighting more. Maybe she just lashed out a little bit, maybe she wants you to talk to her like I do. Did. Just that once." Freddy looks embarrassed, and Tabby feels exhausted.

"But it's—" Tabby doesn't finish the sentence either. It's hard to find words to express the violence underneath it. It's not just Rebecca ganging up on Tabby with her best friend. It's showing Tabby how powerful she is. That she can shape what other people think. That she can make sure they know that it's Tabby who's behaving badly, even when it's her, Rebecca. Trying to make sense of it makes Tabby squirm, it's so hard to pin down. It makes her doubt her own sanity. She just needs someone to say, "*Yes. I see that. I see what she's doing there to you.*" But it sounds so trite, like Tabby is so sensitive. She can't manage to convey the look on her mother's face. The hatred. The fury. And something in her shies away from making it too clear. Like there's something wrong with *her,* Tabby, because perhaps she *is* unlovable.

Because why else would your mother put you down and take such care to show how much she despises you?

"But it happens all the time," she'd said, softly, and could see with absolute clarity that Freddy didn't get it in the slightest.

But not *him.* He might not have seen it in action, but he understood it, even that first time she confided in him. He *understood.* It made her heart soar.

"You poor little duck," he'd said, and he was so genuinely pained for her, and outraged for her, and it was such a relief to finally have someone understand how painful it was, how terrifying, someone who didn't minimize it, or tell her it didn't sound that bad, that when he'd opened his arms to comfort her, she had been overcome with so much relief that she'd fallen into them, and sobbed and sobbed and sobbed. And when he lifted her chin and stared into her eyes and then kissed her, she had never felt so close to anyone her whole entire life.

She would have crawled inside his body to get closer to him if she could.

25

Nancy peers in her daughter's bedroom. It's still dark, the blinds drawn aggressively, despite it being mid-afternoon, and Nancy shifts uneasily in the doorway.

"Freddy? Hon?"

She gets that Freddy is worried about Tabby. They all are. The thought of it all makes her sick to her stomach.

"Honey. Nate's here. He wants to ask you about Tabby. Do you think you could talk to him?"

"No." Freddy sounds wide awake, and her voice is hard. Nancy is taken aback.

"I know you're worried, honey. And I know you wouldn't want to betray any secrets. But you might know something, something small that could help them to find Tabby." Nancy repeats what Nate had said to her, why he was there. She's not entirely comfortable with Nate questioning her daughter—there was that incident on Messenger, Rebecca had mentioned it when Nancy had expressed her condolences about the separation, and she didn't know the details, but it sounded like Nate had done something creepy online to a woman, enough for the marriage to break down over it—but she thinks about if the roles were reversed, and feels a panic so overwhelming she can't do anything but acquiesce.

She would do the same. Talk to anyone who could tell her anything.

Gingerly, she steps into the room and slowly rolls up the blinds, and Freddy curses her. Nancy is even more taken aback.

"Honey. His daughter is missing. Be reasonable. And please don't speak to me like that."

She watches the shape under the doona for a minute, then heads back toward the door. "I'll tell Nate you'll be down in five minutes. Please don't make me come back up."

Downstairs, Nancy smiles apologetically at Nate. "She's been pretty upset. Spending a lot of time in her room. She'll be down shortly. I've asked her though; I don't think she knows anything that could help you. But of course we'll try."

Nancy offers Nate a cup of tea, and he asks if she has any coffee. She nods and turns on their machine.

"How's Gen?"

Nate looks haggard. He often looks tired when Nancy sees him, but she sees him infrequently. Occasionally at school pickup. These days the girls got around on their bikes a lot. She didn't drop Freddy to anyone's house, unless they lived across town.

She had felt sorry for him after the separation, despite whatever it was he'd done. It seemed as though his middle-class life had taken a nosedive. She'd surmised bits and pieces from throw-away lines from Freddy or Tabby, but Nancy was too polite to ask them for any details.

The most important thing was that he was still there for the kids. And Tabby seemed to adore him.

"She's much the same as Freddy I suppose. Teary. Quiet. She called her grandparents. I didn't even know they were in touch. But they've taken her to stay at a hotel. Someone was in the house last night. Going through Tabby's room. The police have dusted for fingerprints, but it seems like there's more going on than Tabby just running away and obviously we want someone to keep Gen safe. Rebecca is estranged from her parents though; it feels weird for them to have Gen."

Nate is rambling, not even really registering Nancy's presence, and her heart skips a beat.

An intruder?

What on earth was Tabby mixed up in?

And she knows it's selfish, and horrible, but as she listens to Nate, all she can think of is how to keep Freddy out of it.

She knew that girl was going to be trouble, dammit.

Freddy was far too nice and loyal. Far too committed to this one friendship. Nancy *knew* she should have pressed more to keep the other friends more involved. But after that one movie night, it had all fizzled out again. There was only Tabby.

"Nate."

Freddy is wearing her father's jumper. It hangs down to her knees, and she looks tiny and child-like. She doesn't quite meet Nate's eyes.

"Freddy. Sweetheart. How are you? This must all be so upsetting for you." Nancy is grateful to see that the sight of Freddy has pulled him out of himself a little. He looks genuinely worried, and a little bit shocked at how different Freddy looks. Nancy hopes he'll be gentle with her, and is sticking close to intervene if he is not.

"Fine." Freddy is short, sitting on the edge of a barstool as far away from Nate as she can be.

She pokes the toe of one slipper repeatedly into the island bench. It makes a dull tapping sound.

"I know it's hard for friends, I know you probably have secrets and things you don't want to tell me. But this is very serious. We need to find Tabby. She might be in danger. So anything you know that might help us is really, really important. Like…" Nate hesitates. "We think she had an older boyfriend, but we don't know who it was. Could you tell me, Freddy, please?"

Here Freddy looks up, a spark of anger in her eyes, and Nancy is shocked for the third time that morning. "What makes you think she'd tell me?" she spits. "She's been moody and shitty with me for months."

Nate looks taken aback too. "Really? You're the only friend she seems to have kept in touch with. She always speaks so highly of you."

For a second Freddy looks young and hopeful, like she's straining toward something in Nate's words, but her face closes off again immediately. "Well, pity she didn't treat me like it. She's been bloody horrible, if you must know. Inviting me over then kicking me out. You can ask Mrs. G," she adds, as though Nate might doubt her. "I spoke to her about it one day after Tabby kicked me out and wouldn't tell me why." Freddy looks down again, and kicks the wall of the bench harder. "Anyway, I heard the door was open. No one broke in. You have a key, right, Nate? Maybe you were there that night. Maybe you or Leroy were the ones she was running away from."

"Freddy!" Nancy is mortified. She has never heard Freddy speak to an adult like that in her life. "That is not okay! You can't just throw around accusations like that!"

"It's okay, it's okay." Nate is looking at Freddy with a worried expression. He wants to know if Freddy knew that he was at the house on Sunday night, and if so, how, or if she was just throwing random thoughts out there, but asks, "So you think she ran away? And she might run *from* Leroy? Not with Leroy?" He desperately doesn't want to sound like a paranoid dad, but anything Freddy can tell him about Tabby's relationship with Leroy is more than anyone else can tell him.

Freddy looks at him pityingly. "I told you. I don't know. She hasn't confided anything in me. But earlier, like months ago, she complained about Leroy a lot. Coming in to her room. Being smarmy. She seemed really angry toward him. And she didn't say anything, but I got the feeling she was seeing someone. But it could be anyone." Freddy gets a faraway look in her eyes, then she looks back at Nate, meeting his eyes for the first time, eyes narrowing. "It's not like she was stuck for choice. She could have bloody anyone she batted her eyelashes at."

For the first time, Nancy wonders if Freddy was jealous of Tabby's beauty. She's never heard her complain or compare, but the way she says that, the bitter edge to her voice, makes her wonder.

Did Tabby get a boy that Freddy liked? Did Tabby betray her?

"What do you mean 'maybe I was at the house that night'? What made you say that, Freddy?" Nate looks deeply uncomfortable, and Nancy wonders about Freddy's accusations. *Was he there that night? Why would Freddy say that? Why did Nate look so guilty about it?* Nate spying on his ex-wife's house *should* make him uncomfortable, she thinks. It was too much of a coincidence, on the night Tabby went missing. Her mind is spinning. *Did Nate see Tabby and Leroy together, and kill Leroy in a fit of protective rage?*

God knows, if some middle-aged man was fooling around with Freddy, she might want to kill them, too.

Freddy hasn't answered Nate. She just keeps kicking the island bench, eyes narrowed.

"Are you angry with her, Freddy? I thought you guys were really close, but it seems like you're angry with her about something." Nate looks confused. This is not how he thought this conversation would go. He expected Freddy to be reluctant to talk to him, to have to work hard to draw secrets out of her. He didn't expect he'd have to deflect her outright hostility.

Nancy is confused, too.

"What about enemies?" Nate goes on. "She got a nasty text message on her phone a few days ago. The police will probably be able to trace the number," Nate lies, hoping to fast-track Freddy sharing who might have sent it. "You don't know who might have been angry with her, do you?" *Besides you*, he thinks to himself, and glances at Nancy, wondering if she's thinking the same thing.

Freddy looks uneasy. "She's not really been talking to many people. Like I told you, she's been moody. Doesn't want to do anything. But... Trent took her dumping him pretty hard. It could be him. Especially if he found out she'd replaced him."

"How would he find out?" Nate presses. "No one else seems to know. Not even Gen."

"Maybe you should ask Rebecca," Freddy shoots back, sarcastically.

"Freddy!" Nancy says again, exasperated. "What has gotten into you?"

"Well, she was always complaining about Rebecca, picking on her. She sounded like a wimp, to be honest. Like Rebecca would say something mean and she'd cry for days. It's not like she's the only person to fight with her parents." Freddy shoots Nancy a look which neither Nate nor Nancy can interpret.

"We don't really fight, do we, sweetheart? Like, have you ever been upset with me for days?"

Something in Freddy softens when she looks at her mother. "No, Mom," she says. "Maybe I'm just mad at her for being so flakey recently. It's almost like she started doing to me what she complained her mom did to her. Picking on me for no reason. Saying shitty things." Here Freddy looks almost embarrassed, and Nate and Nancy exchange glances.

"Can I go now?"

"Sure." Nate watches Freddy slip out of the room. He's thrown by her animosity. *Did Tabby steal a boy she liked? Did she send the message?*

But no, Freddy's number was in Tabby's phone. And he's sure Nancy and Fred wouldn't have bought their only child a burner phone. They seem to dote on her. Not the way that Rebecca dotes, with expensive gifts and a shiny veneer, but actually really spending time with her.

He remembers once, years ago, having them round for dinner with Rebecca. Things were still good with Rebecca then, they'd had a lovely night. And Nate had watched the way both Fred and Nancy spoke to the girls, like they were really interested in their thoughts, their passions.

He'd thought the two families would start hanging out more, but it had never happened again, though he can't remember why.

"Was Freddy here on Sunday night?" Nate asks Nancy, his brow furrowed. "We know Tabby went out. She got home about ten. I guess she maybe met her boyfriend. We can't find any information on her phone, where she was, who she was with. Then she must have left again after midnight." Nate reddens, thinking about how he knows that, sitting watching the house. He wonders if Nancy can see through him, if she now knows that, too.

"Gen says she had a second phone. That's weird, right? Freddy only has one phone, right?"

Nancy looks at him strangely, and nods. She looks distracted. "So she was keeping secrets," she muses. "A second phone is to hide who you're talking to."

Nate nods forlornly. "I just wish she'd come to me. Told me what was going on. Because if a boy is texting her on a secret phone, he's got something to hide, too, right?"

He pauses, though. Because Tabby had come to him, hadn't she? She'd asked to move in with him, and been weird when he turned her down.

He should have realized that things were bad at home.

How bad, though?

What did it drive Tabby to?

What had she done?

26

Six Weeks Earlier

Nate sits outside Rebecca's house, his hands thrumming on the steering wheel.

He turns the engine off, and braces himself.

Then he shakes his head, and switches the ignition back on, muttering curses.

He should get this over with.

His palms are clammy, his breathing shallow. He leans back, closes his eyes, tries to take deep breaths. Familiar feelings of anger compete with his nervousness.

It's not practical for the kids to live with him.

He wonders if it's just Tabby who is thinking about it, or if Gen is as well. He can't imagine Gen would want to live apart from Tabby. While Tabby is the one everyone's eyes are drawn to, Nate wishes people would pay more attention to his youngest daughter. Quiet, watchful, thoughtful Genevieve.

If Tabby is struggling, Genevieve would be strong enough to lean on.

She was so even-tempered, Genevieve.

Is Tabby struggling?

Nate wonders why she has asked to live with him now. She's seemed happy the last few months. Back to her normal self, really. Ever since that little hiccup with Trent and her poor grades, Nate hasn't seen anything to worry about. She ditched the boy and settled back in to study. If anything, she's been working even harder than before.

He should talk to Rebecca about it. That's why he's here. Because, deep down, he knows why Tabby might want to leave Rebecca's house. It's the same reason he wanted to leave. He's kidded himself all this time that he was the only target of Rebecca's rages; that she's mellowed without him there. He's put it in the "too hard" basket, because *mostly* Rebecca is perfectly lovely. You only saw that side of her occasionally. It was so rare that after a while you forgot it even happened. You started to think perhaps you were going mad, that this was normal behavior, that she just lost her temper sometimes. But if he really thought about it, if he really let himself remember... well, there was something very violent about Rebecca in distress.

Something terrifying.

After years with her, he thought he understood it, to some degree. It was about power and control, yes. But that was too simplistic an explanation.

If he really dug in deep around it, he thought it was more to do with pain.

When Rebecca felt hurt or vulnerable, she lashed out.

Well, lashed out was an understatement. *Lost her mind* might be more accurate.

He'd tried to talk to her about it, of course. But it was hard to articulate. It was hard to wrestle with, when you were being told you were wrong all the time.

Gaslit.

Yes. There was a word for it now. Somehow Rebecca managed to twist things around so that he was the one who was in the wrong. That she was just reacting to *his* bad behavior.

That she was justified, even.

It makes his head hurt, even now.

Most people, he thought, you'd have a conversation with. You'd be able to say, "Well, that seemed out of all proportion. That seemed a little bit unhinged. Let's talk about it, let's work it out."

Not Rebecca. It was all his fault, every time. *Couldn't he see how he drove her to it?* And she was so convincing, for a long time he did think it was all his fault. If only he didn't wind her up. If only he remembered to be more respectful. The final straw was when he went out for dinner with his brother, and when he got home Rebecca was nearly frothing at the mouth she was so enraged.

She said he never told her he was going out, but he was sure he had.

She said the kids were distressed and worried about where he was, and she'd had to manage their fears.

She's said if other people were more important than his family, perhaps he should just "fuck off and live with his brother," because she wouldn't put up with being disrespected like this.

And maybe it was because he'd just been outside their little bubble, spending time with his brother, that he could actually see for the first time that she was completely insane, and trying to make *him* feel bad, when he hadn't actually done anything that he ought to feel bad about. Maybe she was trying to make him feel bad about what she was about to do. Her attack, her violence. It made no sense, and he'd had the overwhelming sense that he needed to leave immediately, or he'd be sucked into Rebecca's reality forever and lose himself completely.

And now. Well. Maybe it was nothing, but Tabby asking to move in with him, the way she asked, the *vulnerability* of it. Any other teenager fighting with their mom would be angry, state the reasons why they wanted to leave. Unreasonable bedtimes. Conflict over screen time. But not Tabby. Just a fearful little question, then the pretense that it didn't matter.

But it did.

He didn't want to talk to Rebecca. He really, really didn't. He knew exactly how the conversation would go. The *reasonableness* of it. How he'd end up doubting himself. How smug and superior and *kind* she would be. Helping him to get a better perspective. Listing all the evidence that she's Mom Extraordinaire.

His stomach churns, and he knows he's sweating, dark patches probably visible under his arms.

He doesn't want to get out of the car.

Maybe he'll wait till Tuesday, ask Tabby a bit more about it. Try to get some more information, some concrete facts to arm himself with.

He hesitates for a moment, then convinces himself that this is really the only sensible option, the *safest* option for both Tabby and him.

Then he puts the car into gear and drives away.

27

THE LITTLE GIRL IS EXHAUSTED.

She doesn't really understand what the fights are about. Her mother is furious with her father, or is her father furious with her mother? It swings like a pendulum, one way then another, over and over again.

Anger. Shouting. Cruelty to everyone.

Do other families fight like this?

She has a plan though. And even though she didn't get much sleep last night—she knows she shouldn't listen, she knows that, but she's just trying to understand, just trying to find some way she can help them, help herself—she's still going to follow through with it. She's buoyed by excitement, of the potential of her plan to make a difference.

They weren't always like this, and she knows if she tries hard enough, she can make things go back to the way they were.

She's ten years old, and she has no idea how little difference her intended plan will make.

The actual outcome though? That will make a difference.

Not the difference she had hoped for. But a difference that will reverberate around her forever.

Her parents seem so fed up. Like they don't even want to see their children, let alone have to look after them. Perhaps if they have a bit of space, they might find something nice to talk about? Without her and her sister here, mucking things up, getting in the way, making them angry. Maybe they'll smile at each other, with crinkly eyes, and maybe even hold hands or kiss a little bit?

The little girl has seen that, she remembers it. She remembers more love in their house, once. She is sure she remembers it.

So when her mother comes in and opens the blinds—not saying anything, no "good morning," nothing—she jumps out of bed with unusual enthusiasm.

She tugs on her sister's doona, smiling at her, kissing her forehead.

"Bubba, bubba," she whispers, smoothing her hair, kissing each eyelid. "Get up! I have a surprise for you today. It's going to be wonderful."

And it is wonderful, for a little while.

And then the plan goes pear-shaped and nothing is wonderful, ever again.

28

Nate opens the door to a crying Genevieve. Cheryl looks apologetic.

"She wanted to come back. She can't tell me what's wrong."

Nate picks Genevieve up, her small body limp against him, and beckons Cheryl inside. Rob is nowhere to be seen, and Nate doesn't ask.

"Is there any news? Rebecca hasn't returned my calls."

Nate glances at Cheryl. It seems to be a statement of fact, rather than said with any resentment, but he wonders about it. Rebecca had told him that she'd check in with Gen, who doesn't have a personal phone yet.

How would she check in, without calling Cheryl or Rob?

"Yes. They've ruled Leroy's cause of death as drowning. There was some blunt force trauma to his head, but they think it's consistent with falling off the bridge onto the rocks below. They think it knocked him out and so he drowned." Nate wonders whether he should be conveying this in front of Genevieve, but he supposes she'll find out anyway. It's better to hear it in his arms than elsewhere. She doesn't actually seem to have heard though, and is a dead weight around his neck.

He carries her into the lounge room and places her gently on the couch. "Gen, honey? How are you? You wanna talk to me?" Nate kneels down in front of her, but Gen leans backward into the couch, her eyes closed.

"I just want everything to go back to normal," she says softly, not opening her eyes. Nate rubs her legs gently.

What was normal, in this family?

"Leroy was just trying to help her, you know." Genevieve keeps her eyes firmly closed, and Nat stops the motion of his hand on her legs.

"How so?" he asks softly.

"You know," she replies, still refusing to look at him. Nate's heart skips a beat.

"Rebecca?" he asks, and Genevieve nods, imperceptible.

"Fighting?" Nate is watching her carefully. He doesn't look at Cheryl.

"Does fighting apply to it, Dad?" Genevieve sounds tired and frustrated. Disappointed, even. Like Nate should know better.

He should know better. He should have done better.

"She fought with Tabby like she fought with me?" His voice is very soft, searching Genevieve's face. Cheryl is forgotten. All Nate can see is how he's let his children down.

Gen gives a tiny nod, and Nate leans forward into her, his arms coming around her fiercely. "Why didn't you tell me?" he whispers, but immediately wants to take it back. "It's not your job. I should have known. I should have asked. I'm sorry, Gen. I'm sorry. I'm sorry."

"What do you mean? What's going on?" Cheryl's voice is shrill, panicked, intruding into this quiet space where Nate just wants to hold his daughter, find a way to tell her how sorry he is. But Genevieve sits up and looks at them both with a defeated look on her face, like she's thirty-four, not fourteen.

Like she's lived a long, hard life.

"Mom's just really mean sometimes, Grandma. She's so mean to Tabby it makes me want to die."

Nate rocks back on his heels, staring at Gen. He and Cheryl are so shocked the silence is absolute. For a moment nobody moves, then Gen whispers, "I just wanted it to stop."

Nate can hear his own heartbeat thudding in his ears.

"What happened, Gen?" he says, his voice urgent, but Gen starts to sob, and Nate can't make out her words through the great wracking sobs tearing through her. He bites his lip, hard, and tastes blood, trying not to shake his daughter, some unspecified terror filling him, wanting to look after her, comfort her, but needing to know, right now, what she is talking about.

"You've got to tell me, Gen," he whispers. "What happened? What did you do?"

29

One Month Earlier

"Would you run away with me if my mother kicked me out?"

Tabby is lying naked, her long legs thrown casually over her lover's stomach. They're in a cheap hotel on a Saturday afternoon. Tabby misses her work at Miss Ambrosia, but it was the only time her lover could meet her safely, so it was a price she was willing to pay.

She really wants to go out for lunch, or see a movie, and to be honest she's getting sick of just meeting in hotel rooms and making love, but she doesn't doubt that the rest will come, sooner or later.

Hopefully sooner.

"Of course," he tells her, smiling. "Just try not to get kicked out yet. There're a few things I need to finalize before we can be together."

"In public. Like a proper couple."

"Yep," he says, reaching over and stroking a breast. His eyes wander down the length of her to her crotch, and something about it irritates Tabby.

She brushes his hand away. They've already had sex twice today. She wants to talk about their future.

"Will we get our own place?"

He hesitates, dragging his eyes back up to hers. "We'll get our own place. It would be weird, otherwise, don't you think? Moving in to the marital bed?"

"Yeah." Tabby smiles sleepily. "I just can't wait, you know. I know you want me to finish school, but I can do that wherever I'm living. In fact I'll probably do better if it's just you and me. Without my mother around ruining everything." Darkness flits across her face, and across his, too.

"There's no rush, is there? We get to spend every Saturday together, like this." He squeezes a breast again, and Tabby can see he's hard again already. "Plus, the other times, which just make it more exciting. When we see each other, but can't be together. It drives me crazy."

"I'm sick of waiting," Tabby says, petulant. "What does it matter if it's now or later? Can't you just sort everything out now?"

"Not if you want to have a nice house, honey. I have to work out the money. I have to do all that before we go public, or it might make things difficult."

"I don't care about money! We could live in a caravan for all I care."

"I know, I know. If I had you, it would nearly be enough." His voice is soothing, pulling Tabby against him, kissing her forehead, her cheek, slowly making his way down to a nipple. "But I've worked a long time to get where I am. I don't want to start again with nothing. You'll have to trust me, Tab. Just give it a little more time."

Tabby starts to say something, but it's lost amongst his moans, and he pushes a finger into her mouth, climbing on top of her, the thought of houses and cohabiting far, far from his mind, which is fully occupied with her lush young body, and the space between her legs.

LATER, Tabby eyes the lock on her door.

A plan has started to hatch in her mind.

At first, the thought of fleeing was enough. She couldn't think of much else, if she was honest. There was Freddy still hanging on her every word, and it irked Tabby in a way she couldn't articulate. Nothing she said or did seemed to get rid of Freddy. And she felt bad, but she just didn't feel that way about her friend. When Freddy was there, she couldn't wait to get rid of her.

She wanted to cut ties, to be free.

At the same time, she knows she reels Freddy back in. When she feels low, or unloved, she knows that Freddy will boost her mood. She reaches out to her, mopey, an unasked question, and Freddy is there for her every time. Always answering that question, in a roundabout way.

You're loved.

Why Freddy loves her so much is a mystery to Tabby. She knows she hasn't been a very good friend.

She pushes her guilt aside though.

She just wants to leave, to start her new life.

And she just has this little idea of how to get that ball rolling.

Idly, she flips open her phone.

30

ONE DAY Earlier

"Do you remember that time at the snow?"

"Yeah."

Genevieve is lying on Tabby's bed. Tabby is getting ready to go to work.

"It was like... I don't know what it was like."

"Yeah." Genevieve doesn't want to talk about her mother anymore. She knows Tabby is just trying to justify wanting to leave. She knows why Tabby wants to leave. She wants to leave too.

She definitely doesn't want to be left alone with her mother.

"He's not going to leave her for you, Tabby. He's lying to you."

Tabby turns on her, her face fierce, her eyes wild. "Don't say that!" she shouts. "He loves me! And I'm sorry you're being left behind, I really am, but it never happens to you! I'm the one who's stuck with her! If you don't want to stay here without me, go live with Dad!"

Genevieve's eyes fill with tears. "You said he said no." Her voice is small. She feels terrified. Without Tabby, she has no ally, no protector, no confidant.

Without Tabby, the world seems to tilt off axis, like they might all just slide and scrape and tumble right off the edge of the earth, and float off into space, untethered and weightless and destined to die.

It's not just selfishness, though. Genevieve thinks Tabby has no clue. Tabby feels loved, thinks she is loved, but she has no idea just how much her beauty drives men to distraction. Genevieve has been watching it for years. Tabby's attractiveness makes men lose their minds.

Once, Genevieve had been jealous of it. No one ever paid her so much attention. No one ever stopped to stare at her in wonder.

But now, Genevieve sees it's a double-edged sword. Somehow, she thinks that Rebecca's rage is linked to Tabby's beauty. She can't understand how, or why, but it's the only explanation that she can come up with which explains why she, Gen, is spared, and Tabby is not.

And then, on top of all that pain and stress, boys want Tabby for the wrong reasons. Like Trent, that drip. Gen would see them together, and could see that Trent was not interested in talking to Tabby, in understanding her deeply. He was utterly preoccupied with showing her off, and keeping her to himself. Every time she saw them in the schoolyard together, Gen wanted to walk right up to Trent and punch him in the face.

Her heart hurts for her sister. Partly because she knows that Tabby is so loveable, just for herself. Her beauty is a distraction, it's not the main thing. Men should choose her because she's marvelous, not because she's beautiful. But Genevieve doesn't think that's how it works for Tabby. And it's not fair, and it's not right, but it's also just the way it is.

Tabby is going to find out eventually, and she is going to be devastated.

But Genevieve can help her.

Genevieve can fix this.

It's going to hurt, and Tabby is going to be angry, but she'll realize eventually.

She'll come back around.

"I love you, Tab," she says now, watching her sister with a heavy heart.

Waiting patiently for her to leave for work so she can put her plan into action.

Disappearance Day

"Where have you been?"

Tabby stops in the doorway. Rebecca is sitting at the kitchen table, in the dark.

"Just studying," Tabby replies. Her heart starts to beat faster.

That wasn't true. She had, in fact, just been riding around. She'd hoped she could convince *him* to come out and meet her, but he couldn't get away, and she didn't want to go home. She'd ridden, aimlessly, till the dark and the cold had made even home seem more attractive.

Now, hairs prickling on her neck, she thinks the dark and the cold seem like the better option.

Maybe tonight? she thinks to herself. But now that she's faced with the possibility, she feels twisted with fear. Thinking about something, alone with her anger, her sense of betrayal, is different from taking action while her mother looms large in the dark.

Charlie runs to her, her voice waking him from where he

had been sleeping in his basket up the hall. She bends down to pat him, making cooing noises, as though to a child.

"Who's my favorite little baby, hey bubba boo," she says, making kissing noises, and she can feel the change in the air, which was tense anyway, like her words have drifted out there and poked and stabbed at something, electric.

What was Rebecca angry about now?

This didn't fit the pattern. She was home by curfew. She was just patting her dog. Nothing here should tip her mother over the edge.

Tabby slows her patting, tries to keep her movements calm and slow. As though it might be contagious, as though Rebecca might be calmed by it herself.

Inexplicably, she feels like crying.

Couldn't Rebecca just be happy to see her for once? Couldn't she just say hello and give her a hug, like Nancy does with Freddy?

The thought of Nancy and Freddy makes Tabby jump.

Everything feels terrible.

She doesn't want Rebecca to see her cry. She knows it changes things, it makes Rebecca gentle, but it's not real, it's not true. She can't trust it, she can't lean in to it. She can't be fooled into thinking it changes anything. It doesn't matter what she does, if she's angry and mean, or teary and vulnerable. In the end, whenever she shares herself with Rebecca, the only end point is ever rage. Like all roads lead to the one place.

Tabby takes a deep breath, then smiles at her mother in the gloom. She doesn't want to provoke her, not tonight. She just wants to go to bed.

"How was your night, Mom?" she asks, trying to be disarming, trying to win her mother over. "Are Gen and Leroy in bed?"

"Yes. Which is where I would be, too, if I didn't have to sit up worrying about you."

Seconds tick by between them, strained and dark. Tabby

tries to think about what to do, but it's so hard to think once adrenaline has kicked in. Her heart pounds, she can't even hear properly. Every muscle in her body strains, without a destination. She doesn't know where to run to, where to hide.

She strokes Charlie's ears methodically, thoughtlessly. "Hey little bubba, little one," she murmurs, trying to think, trying to buy time to come up with a better plan. But she can feel Rebecca lean forward, in the darkness.

"You love that bloody dog more than you love me," she hisses, and Tabby feels something shift inside her, and maybe it has to be tonight, maybe she can't stand this insanity for one more single second.

"So what if I do?" she says coolly, one hand reaching for the light switch, the other reaching for her phone.

As Rebecca's chair scrapes backward on the kitchen tiles, Tabby takes a deep breath, and hits record.

THE SUN IS BRIGHT, *and the little girl is filled with happiness.*

It's random, and she knows it will be fleeting, but in that moment there is sunshine and hope and her heart swells with something uncontainable.

Her mother will be so proud.

She's done well at her swimming lessons.

Like everything she does, she works hard. She puts all of her efforts into it. She can now swim a whole lap of the pool, her little legs working overtime.

She can't keep up with the other kids, but they've all been having lessons for years, her teacher tells her.

She'll catch up.

Now, she hugs her little sister. "Bubba boo, bubba boo," she coos, beaming at her, taking her hand.

Her exhaustion from the sleepless night is forgotten under her excitement, her special secret. Her sister will be so happy! She wants to do everything her big sister does, she hates being left behind, being left out of things. She hasn't been allowed to have swimming lessons. Her mother can't get her to class, it's earlier than Rebecca's, it's during work hours, it's too hard.

It's Rebecca's job to teach Moira how to swim.

Her mother doesn't know it, but she is going to teach her today.

She imagines her mother's face when she gets home, when she tells her, "Moira can swim! I taught her today!" She imagines the pride, the thanks she will get.

She's made careful notes of the important things her teacher has told her. She doesn't have floaties or kickboards, but she will make do.

She's always managed to make do. She's a remarkably resourceful girl—her teachers have told her that on many occasions.

Now, she holds Moira's hand carefully as they wade into the river. She's overflowing with excitement—that she can share this lovely thing with her sister, who is her best friend, even though she's four years younger. She's so adorable, so sweet, so lovely to cuddle. Her little love. Her little bubba boo.

But the excitement is also because she might manage to please her mother, and she glows with pride in anticipation.

The water is colder than she expected, and Moira makes a little whimpering sound, and tugs on her hand as though to back out, go backward up the riverbank, and Rebecca feels a moment of frustration. She doesn't want a little bit of cold water to ruin her plans.

She frowns at Moira, one hand coming to her hip. "Just for a little bit, Moira. Please?" And Moira looks at her uncertainly, because she wants to please her sister, but it's very cold, and suddenly the moving water looks scary to Moira, not exciting. She can see a leaf whipping past in the current, gone in seconds, and involuntarily she steps backward, back up the bank.

And Rebecca says her name in frustration, and gives her hand a little tug.

She only wanted to halt her backward motion, she didn't mean anything else by it, she wasn't trying to pull her in, she wouldn't force her. But she gives her sister's hand a little tug, and she steps back as she does so to balance herself, but the ground drops away beneath her and she falls backward, holding on to her sister's hand, yanking her forward, and they both fall into the river, where it is very dark and very cold.

33

ONE DAY Earlier

In Tabby's room, Genevieve moves methodically.

She doesn't know what she's searching for, but she knows she will find it. Tabby is too creative, too emotional to have not left some trace of her affair inside this room.

She's careful not to disturb anything, and is fast and silent. It doesn't take her long to find the sketchbook. She flips through it fast, occasionally glancing at the locked door.

For a moment, she's distracted by what she sees. Tabby's talent exceeds all her expectations. Charlie grins out at her, his tongue lolling.

There's one of Rebecca, in that space between normal and enraged. Her face looks vulnerable, child-like. It passes so quickly it would barely register for most people. If you weren't paying attention.

If you didn't need to pay attention, if you didn't need to be hypervigilant for what came after.

Tabby has caught it perfectly.

Something catches in Genevieve's throat.

It's just painful enough for them to never quite be able to

hate her. Even at fourteen, Genevieve can see that her fury hides something darker and more painful in herself. Something that, once touched upon, she tries to bury under exerting a power so large it squashes them down and raises her up.

Gen might keep her friends away from her mother. She might have grown quiet and watchful. But children never stop straining toward their parents' love.

Gen sees that sketch and yearns toward Rebecca. Wants to burrow into her and make her feel better. She knows that won't make Rebecca feel better. But she wants to do it anyway.

She pushes her feelings aside, though, and flips through sketch after sketch until she finds what she's looking for. Then she carefully puts everything back in its place and takes the sketchpad to her own room. She doesn't yet know what she is going to do with it. She just instinctively wants to hide it somewhere safe.

Then she opens her phone, and sends Freddy a message.

She thinks Freddy will fix it.

And make it all go away.

She thinks of it like a problem to solve, where x plus y equals something predictable, something known.

She tells Freddy that Tabby is having an affair with Fred.

Freddy will want it to stop, too.

Tabby will listen to Freddy, where she didn't listen to Genevieve.

For all her wisdom beyond her years, and all the thought she has put into this, though, her thinking is still the thinking of a child. All she can think about is the end point. Other outcomes, and collateral damage, do not even enter her mind.

34

DISAPPEARANCE DAY

You've got to help me.

Tabby's hands are shaking as she types, she can barely tap the letters out. Her breath is coming in shuddering sobs. She checks the lock again, checks the window.

Please. You've got to get me tonight. I need you tonight.

Then she panics more, realizing she's used the wrong phone, and deletes the messages, her hands shaking. She fumbles for her old maths textbook. She's cut a hollow out inside it, tucked her secret phone inside. She mistypes the code twice before unlocking it.

Sorry, sorry, she types, hesitating, wondering if he'd be mad that she used the wrong phone. Anyone could link that number to her.

Please. You've got to help me. I'm scared. She killed him. She killed him.

Here Tabby doubles over in pain. She was so stupid. She had thought she was in control now, that her mother couldn't hurt her. She can't shake the image from her mind. The satisfaction in her eyes, the sly little smile. The casual way she'd reached out and grabbed the dog. Not taking her eyes off Tabby.

Tabby had always thought that Rebecca lost control, that that's how she could be so vile, so awful. But tonight she saw something else entirely.

That look.

She was completely in control. She *chose* to do that. She wasn't out of control. She knew absolutely, utterly, what she was doing.

Snap.

He hadn't even made a sound.

Tabby circles in her room, beside herself. *Did he feel it? Did it hurt?*

She looks out her window. It's not that high.

No answer.

I'm coming now, she types, bugger waiting, bugger timelines, bugger all of it. She killed my dog. You said you loved me. Well, I need you now. I can't stay here. I'm scared. She's crazy.

Tabby throws a few things in her backpack. She can't think clearly. She can't imagine what will happen. She just needs to get out of this house.

Genevieve.

She stops packing things abruptly.

She can't leave Genevieve. Oh God.

She thinks of Charlie's little body in the kitchen, and stifles a sob.

Was that a footstep outside her door?

Rebecca has never hurt her. Never laid a hand on her. She didn't have to. She could bring Tabby to her knees with a glance, a look in her eye.

She'd gotten complacent. She never thought Rebecca would *actually* hurt anyone. Not physically. But that look on her face. She was completely insane. She'd completely blanked out, gone somewhere else. Somewhere where she could kill their dog with just the flick of her wrist.

She can't leave Genevieve.

Tabby, Jesus. You can't come here. Just wait till tomorrow. Or call your Dad.

She'd tried to call Fred then, but he'd cancelled the call on the first ring.

You said you loved me. Well I need you now. I'm coming over, or it's over between us.

She flings the phone down on her bed, the sobs unstoppable. She hates having to force him, she knows it will make him angry, but if he can't help her now, what does their love even mean?

But even as she's flinging clothes into her backpack, the sound of a text message stills her. She doesn't want to look. Somehow, tonight, she's seeing things with peculiar clarity.

He won't let me come.

She knows it before she even looks at her phone.

DON'T YOU DARE, the text reads. And then: Fine then. We're done.

35

ONE DAY Earlier

Freddy screams into her pillow.

Screams and screams and screams.

"Are you all right, honey?" Nancy is knocking on her door, concerned.

The pillow didn't muffle much of anything, then.

She can't talk to her mother now.

She just needs to think. She needs to come up with a plan.

How could she? How could she, how could she, how could she?

This is worse than being rejected. This is excruciating. This is hurting not just Freddy, but Nancy.

This is bigger than her.

Rage rises up in Freddy's chest, not just the rage of the rejected, but the rage of the fooled.

Tabby had misled her. Willingly, extensively. For months. She'd pretended to be her friend, all the while laughing at her, and fucking her father.

She must think she is so thick, so slow, so unimaginative. Was she laughing at her this whole time?

Freddy has never felt so stupid in all her life. But more than that, it's the thought of Nancy that twists something deep inside her. The pain is unbearable.

It's one thing for Tabby to make a fool out of her. But Nancy, who is so gentle, so lovely. Freddy can't even imagine how Nancy will respond to such a thing.

Her whole life feels ruined, in one small text.

Like everything she believed in has been yanked away and lit on fire right in front of her eyes.

She can't bear it. She can't. She needs to make it go away. She needs to fix it, or else take this pain and rage and fury and put it somewhere else.

And as she lies in bed and hatches a plan, the unbearable thing becomes bearable.

Like a million people before her, she takes her pain and turns it into something else.

36

Leroy rubs his eyes. He looks over at his wife. She's breathing evenly. She looks peaceful.

He reaches for his phone, wondering who was texting him so late. He makes a mental note again to switch his settings to night mode. He hates getting woken up, but he keeps forgetting to look up how to change this setting.

Sighing, he touches the home button, the screen lighting up and blinding him. He blinks at it sightlessly for a moment.

Tabby.

God, six messages.

He swings his legs out of bed, unsettled. She never texts him.

Yawning, he opens up his messages, then sits ups straighter, wide awake. He glances at Rebecca, checks she's still sleeping, his heart hammering in his chest, panic prodding him out of bed, down the hallway. He knocks on Tabby's door softly. He doesn't want to wake Rebecca. There's no answer, and he tries the handle.

Locked.

"Tabby, it's me. Jesus Christ. Open up," he whispers, but the house is completely silent. If Tabby's in there, she's holding her breath.

Leroy pads down the other way toward the kitchen. He starts the video back up again. He stopped it in the bedroom, not wanting to wake Rebecca, and besides, the text messages told him all he needed to know.

She killed him. She killed him.

He watches the video and thinks he's going to be sick.

What has he done? For the love of God.

Kind words. A lock on the door.

What the fuck was he thinking?

He grabs his keys, walks quickly back to Tabby's door, puts the key in the lock. It's labeled "work locker" to keep Rebecca from noticing it.

Tabby's room is empty, the window wide open.

A phone he's never seen before is lying on her bed, and the last message still lights up when he pushes the power button.

Fine then. I'm sorry. Meet me at the Tandy Bridge.

Leroy doesn't notice her usual phone, lying where it fell on the floor after she had texted him. But he grabs the second phone, and creeps into his bedroom, finding his jeans and a jumper, trying to be as quiet as possible. But Rebecca sits up, a strange expression on her face.

"What's going on, Leroy?"

And he's so angry, he can't think of what to say to her, rage working across his face as he yanks on his boots.

"You, Rebecca. You're what's going on. You said you'd fix it. And I believed you. Jesus Christ. I've been colluding with you, and your abuse."

And he stalks out of the room and out the front door.

On the veranda, Leroy paces up and down, calling Tabby's number, but it goes straight to voicemail, and he curses, shutting his phone, opening it again. He searches for the bridge in his map app, then goes back inside, slamming the door behind him.

He tries to wake Genevieve, but she's dead to the world, and he's torn.

Can he leave her here, with Rebecca?

But Rebecca's never fought with Gen, he reasons to himself. *And Gen won't even stir before he's back.*

He stands at her bedroom door, stepping away, hesitating. Rebecca appears behind him.

"I'm going to find Tabby," he hisses at her, disgust on his face. "If you hurt that child, I will bloody kill you, do you understand?" And he stalks away from her, out of the house.

He doesn't notice that the door doesn't shut properly behind him, and slowly creaks open as he strides furiously to his car, and tears off into the night.

37

THURSDAY

After the flurry of phone calls, Nate and Cheryl sit at the kitchen table, facing each other awkwardly.

"Detective Casey is going to interview Fred." Nate feels constantly nauseous. He wants to go round there and beat the man to a pulp. His hands have not stopped shaking.

He can't get on to Rebecca. Her phone is on the table beside them, in fact. He can't understand how she could just go walking without her phone while their child is missing.

He wants to blame her for Tabby and Fred, he wants to shout at her and throw things, but he also can barely think through the roar in his ears.

Wrong, wrong, wrong, wrong, wrong.

He had Leroy all wrong. Leroy was the only one trying to help Tabby. He stands up suddenly and rushes to the sink, but just leans over it, saliva dripping from his mouth. No vomit comes.

When he's sure he's not going to be sick, he drinks some water, then goes and sits opposite Cheryl. She's twisting a scarf around and around in her fingers.

"Casey asked us to wait here. She'll call when she's spoken to Fred. She wants to talk to Rebecca."

They've left Genevieve on the couch with a blanket and a DVD. Nate doesn't even know where to start. *How do you talk about the elephant in the room?* He's so agitated, he just wants something to fill the gaping hole where understanding and common sense prevail.

Why is Rebecca like this?

Why is Fred?

Can he even count all the ways in which he has failed?

"What happened to you guys? Why don't you talk?"

Tears slide down Cheryl's face, relentless.

They haven't stopped since Genevieve told them about Fred, and that she'd told Freddy about the affair.

She'd handed him the burner phone. "It was in my room. I don't know how it got there."

"After Moira died—" Cheryl starts, now, and Nate holds up a hand.

"Start there," he says. "I don't know what happened. Only how devastated Rebecca was."

Cheryl starts to sob harder.

"She was only six. Rebecca was ten. Rob and I had had a bad year. I'd had an affair." Nate startles, but Cheryl's eyes are distant, unfocused.

"We were fighting a lot. We put a lot of pressure on Rebecca. She did a lot of the caring for Moira. God, she loved her sister." At this point, Cheryl leans over until her forehead is resting against the table. Her shoulders shake violently.

Nate stares at her, a lump forming in his throat. Everything seems like it is happening in slow motion.

"We were shit parents, I admit that. All we did was fight, and ignore them. I was so lost. Rob was so angry. I don't know how we survived, to be honest." Cheryl is still talking to the table, her voice muffled through her tears. Nate can't see her face.

"It was only a year, I swear. We just weren't paying attention. And I'd told Rebecca she would teach Moira to swim. I didn't mean for her to take her somewhere. I meant, in the local pool, some time later, after Rebecca learnt. She'd only just started lessons herself." Cheryl sits up suddenly, her mouth gaping, her eyes pleading for Nate to understand. "But we didn't explain properly. We didn't. I don't even remember that year, I drank too much, I just wished the kids would leave me alone. I was lost myself. My marriage was falling apart. I didn't know how to fix anything. I thought the kids would just...always be there. That I could get back to mothering later, when I'd sorted out the rest of my life. But of course you can't stop. You can't take time out of parenting. You're there, or you're not."

Cheryl raises her eyes here, looks at Nate directly. He thinks that she thinks she's taking responsibility for herself, her own actions. Not trying to hide, not trying to deflect blame. But he feels her words like little stabs into his flesh.

"Rebecca took her to the river. She was just trying to please me. She was trying to be a good girl. She was always such a good girl. She always tried so hard, at everything. And then. Well. She wouldn't talk about it. All she ever said was that she was teaching her to swim. But I know why she was doing it. She was trying to please me. She was trying to be good."

Cheryl's head sags again. Tears slide silently down her cheeks. Nate gets the sense that they are infinite; that she will never be done crying about this.

"Someone saw them fall in, and they pulled Rebecca out. She could swim enough to resurface, to kick up. But they couldn't see Moira. They didn't find her for two days."

Nate can't imagine. He can't begin to.

"We pulled ourselves together. We tried to support her. She saw a counsellor. But she refused to talk about it. She got so angry whenever we tried to talk about. We tried to tell her it was our fault, that it wasn't her fault, but she'd just scream and scream. And eventually we stopped trying. We thought she was coping. She got on with life. She seemed like she was okay. She did well at school. We decided not talking about it was how she coped. But I think it was a front, now. I don't think she was coping at all. I think she was falling apart. And she put herself back together, somehow, but she did it on her own. She had no one to guide her. She wouldn't let anyone in."

Cheryl pauses, examining some distant thought or distant memory. Her face is pale and tight.

"She didn't," Nate whispers. "She never put herself back together. She's not together. She's not all right." But it's as though Cheryl can't even hear him; she's miles away.

"Rob and I saw a counsellor. God knows how we survived. We tried to make it up to her. But when she left home, she went as far away from us as she could. We moved, you know, to be closer to her. Not so close we made her angry. Just to the border. Just close enough to drive. But she cut us off. She didn't want to see us. She didn't want to talk to us. It was like we made her feel bad about Moira, and her way of coping was to cut us out of her life. And we let her, because, I think, we thought we deserved it. Because she might have taken Moira to the river. But every step toward it? Everything that happened that took her there? We might as well have pushed them both in."

38

DISAPPEARANCE DAY

You've got to help me.

Please. You've got to get me tonight. I need you tonight.

On Sunday night, Freddy is watching her father closely.

She still hasn't quite worked out the details of what to do, how to confront Tabby, how to make her hurt as much as she, Freddy, is hurting. The knowledge of the affair is eating away her insides like acid.

But then Tabby texts, and as quickly as Fred tucks his phone away, it was not quick enough.

Freddy was watching like a hawk.

When he disappears into his bedroom and shuts the door, she watches.

When he comes back out and sits in front of the television, she watches. He looks edgy, uncomfortable, or is she imagining it?

She knows from Genevieve that Tabby has a second phone, so she sits, thinking about why Tabby texted from her regular phone to Fred's, when anyone could see the message, anyone could find out who sent it, and wonder why she was texting

Fred, saying that she needed him. Fred is always leaving his phone around. Which you wouldn't do, if you had something to hide, would you?

She wonders if Fred has a second phone.

"I'm going to go read for a bit," she says, and Nancy smiles at her and takes Fred's hand, and her heart squeezes painfully.

Listening for any movement from the lounge room, she goes into her parents' room. Her mother has a great pile of books on her nightstand. If anyone asks, she'll say she's choosing a book.

Then she starts searching for a hidden phone.

In her father's nightstand, in which she's never looked before, there's a half-empty bottle of lube and a giant pink dildo, and she vomits a little bit in her mouth.

Was that for her mother, or did her father fuck Tabby here sometimes?

No, she knows her parents still have regular sex. She hears them often enough—their bedrooms share a wall, and she has already made a mental note that if she ever has kids, to keep her bedroom well away from theirs.

At those times, she puts earplugs in, grimacing, disgusted. Them trying to be quiet is somehow even worse.

For someone who is usually straightforward and uncomplicated, Freddy is remarkably adept at thinking covertly. Her eyes skim across possible hiding places with precision, categorizing places her mother would frequent. Fred's suits—her mother would check to see if they needed dry cleaning. His sock drawer—Nancy would pair and put socks in there.

Her eyes roam around the walk-in wardrobe.

Some dusty-looking accounting textbooks on the top shelf look promising.

She hoists a chair over and pulls them out, one by one, checking for secret chambers.

Someone had described how to make a hiding place inside a book once in class.

Fred would hide a phone somewhere easily accessible, somewhere he'd be able to check it readily, quickly.

Getting a textbook down is hardly surreptitious, but it is somewhere Nancy would never look.

No secret chambers, though.

The en suite, then.

She pulls out drawers, and bingo.

Six or seven old phones.

She checks them all for charge. The last one lights up at her touch.

Hidden in plain sight.

Freddy guesses her father's passcode with ease. It's the same one he uses for everything, even his bank cards.

Idiot.

She reads Tabby's messages, her heart hammering. Then sees her father's final reply, and something strange happens in her abdomen.

Fred was calling it off.

Tabby was so stupid. As if Fred would ever leave his family for a teenager.

For a moment she's flooded with relief that it's over. Later, it will occur to her that it's not over at all. Fred might be calling off the affair, but everything that's left—what he's done, even what sort of a man chooses to hide his wrongdoing rather than help someone he's supposed to care about, who is clearly in deep distress—will not be over for any of them, for a very long time.

But that doesn't occur to her right now.

Right now, she just wants to make sure Tabby knows that it is over. She thinks quickly. She's so full of rage. She wants to see Tabby, tell her everything, tell her how much sex Fred and

Nancy have, how they're sitting on the couch right now holding hands.

How they usually fuck on movie night. Two hours sitting on the couch together, touching.

Tell her what a fool she was, to think Fred would come and rescue her.

She taps quickly into the phone, then slips it in her pocket.

Her father will notice it's missing, but what's he going to say?

He can't say bloody anything, and she'll deal with him later. She tells her parents she's turning in. Then she slips on her sneakers, and jumps nimbly out of her window and walks quickly to the shed to get her bike.

Across town, Tabby's phone pings: Fine then. I'm sorry. Meet me at the Tandy Bridge.

39

THURSDAY

"We need to talk."

Casey tells Nate that she'll be there in twenty minutes. "Where's Rebecca?"

Nate tells her he doesn't know. "She went walking and hasn't returned."

"I'll call her," Casey says, but Nate tells her not to bother—Rebecca has left her phone behind. Casey curses and hangs up without another word.

Rob arrives, his hulking frame somehow comforting to Nate. "We'll sit with Gen," Cheryl tells him. The air is at once heavy and clear between them. At least one piece of the puzzle has fallen into place.

Nate nods once, and waits at the table.

40

Disappearance Day

At the bridge, Tabby and Freddy are fighting.

Freddy shoves Tabby, and Leroy screams to a stop next to them and jumps out of the car.

"Tabby, Jesus. Oh my God." He pulls her into his arms, but she fights him off, sobbing.

Freddy is crying, too.

"You never stopped her," Tabby sobs, hitting Leroy in the chest, her little arms flailing, and she seems to him like a little doll, tiny and vulnerable and like she might break in two with the slightest puff of wind. Leroy is bewildered, trying to fend off Tabby's blows, and Freddy's shoves too.

"Tabby! Calm down, love. Calm down. What's going on? Why are you out here in the middle of nowhere? Why didn't you wake me instead of texting?"

"Because you always take her side! You say you'll try to help me but you never really do! You just stick a Band-Aid over it! Like a lock on the door! Well, how well did that help tonight? What happens when I'm in the kitchen? What happens when Charlie is?" Her voice cracks, and she doubles over, her shoulders shuddering violently, then slowly sinks to the ground.

Leroy squats down beside her, trying to lift her back up.

"Sweetheart, it's cold. Come here." Tabby pushes his hands away though.

"Why are you here, Freddy? And why are you fighting, not helping her? Jesus, did she tell you what happened?" Leroy feels strangely furious with Freddy, that she'd lure Tabby out to the middle of nowhere instead of asking an adult for help.

But Tabby's done that already, hasn't she? Asked for help?

And fat lot of good it did her. Fat lot of help he was.

Leroy takes a deep breath. *So he hasn't helped. So he didn't realize how bad it was. But he can help now.*

His thoughts are interrupted by Freddy though: "Why don't you ask her, the fucking little slut?" she hisses, and yanks a bike off the ground behind her, swinging a leg over, and pedalling furiously away.

Leroy stares after her, shocked. He turns back to Tabby.

"Tabby, honey. I don't understand what's happening with Freddy. But let's go home. Or at least come sit in the car and let's talk about it. I will keep you safe, I promise."

"No!" Tabby screams jumping back to her feet, trying to pummel him with her fists again. "All you ever do is talk about it! You even tell me to 'just go with it'! Just go along with it and pretend I'm the one with the problem! You just try to minimize the fallout, not fix the problem, and now Charlie is dead, and I'm not going back there! I'm not going back to her! You know exactly what she's like, and you've never done anything except try to smooth out the worst of the bumps. You've never even told her she's the problem, not me." Tabby is crying so hard Leroy can barely understand her, and his stomach feels like a brick in his abdomen, because Tabby is exactly right. He remembers that fight as clear as if it was yesterday. Rebecca flying into a rage about something he didn't understand, something so nonsensical it didn't even seem worth exploring. He'd arrived home and caught the tail end of it, Rebecca screaming so much Tabby had fled, had actually run to her room, and when Leroy had gone to her, his approach had been to try to comfort her tears away, not delve into the problem and truly try to understand it. Just pat her on the back, as though that would solve anything. And when Rebecca had poked her head in the door twenty minutes later, he'd explained to Rebecca that Tabby had had a hard day, she was sorry that she'd been snappy. And he'd felt Tabby stiffen beside him, because it was a lie, but it was the quickest way back to calm, back to harmony, and he'd whispered to her "just go with it" and Rebecca had held on to her miffed attitude, but Leroy could see that she felt vindicated, that the fire had gone out of her, that Tabby would be safe then, that everything was okay.

He's done that so many times, and thought that he'd diffused things.

But all he'd done is postpone the next hurricane, he can see that now. Let Rebecca believe she was justified. All he could see was the way to calm her in the moment, not the way to deal with the problem so it didn't happen again, and again, and again.

What an idiot he's been.

His chest feels tight. He grips Tabby's shoulders, tries to look in her eyes. She's like a wild animal, her pain and her fear emanating from her like a cornered rat. Leroy can't help it; he starts to cry. "Listen, Tabby. You're right. I did it all wrong. I thought I was helping, but I didn't fix the problem and the problem isn't you. But I can see that now. I'm going to fix it now, okay? And I'm going to find you somewhere safe to stay." He pauses for a second, fishes out a hanky and blows his nose. He's not used to crying, it feels weird, and wet, and gross.

He's crying not just for Tabby, or for his failures, but for what he's losing too. Because admitting the scale of the issue means his relationship is in danger, too. And whatever she is with Tabby, sometimes, Leroy still loves Rebecca. She's mostly wonderful.

She's always wonderful to him.

"Why are you fighting with Freddy?" Leroy realizes with a shock that he can't think of any other of Tabby's friends he could ask for help, ask for Tabby to stay with for a while. They've all disappeared over the last year. "Why were you meeting her out here?" He can't make sense of what happened with Charlie and Rebecca ending up with Tabby and Freddy fighting on a bridge.

But he can't get an answer out of Tabby. It's like all the fight has gone out of her, and she falls into his arms shaking quietly, and sobs and sobs and sobs.

"I LET FREDDY DOWN."

Tabby is leaning against Leroy, the cold damp asphalt uncomfortable beneath them. She's limp. She suddenly doesn't know why she took all her anger out on Leroy. He, at least, was trying to help. He sucked at it, but he was the only person who noticed how much Rebecca affected her, and tried in his own inept way to intervene.

Where was her dad?

Where was anyone?

"I let you and Gen down," Leroy responds. "But I'm going to work really hard to fix it. Maybe you can fix it with Freddy, too."

Tabby shakes her head. "I don't think so," she says. "I don't think she'll ever forgive me. I don't blame her." She's silent for a minute, then says, "I've lost Freddy. I've lost Charlie." *I've lost Fred,* she thinks, but doesn't share that with Leroy.

Freddy was right.

"You were only good to fuck," she had jeered at Tabby,

recounting all the times she'd heard her parents making love, all the sex toys she'd found. "Dad doesn't care about you, don't you get it? He got your messages and went and cuddled up with Mom on the couch to watch a movie. He didn't give you another thought. He doesn't know where you are and he doesn't care."

"But he said to meet me here," Tabby had cried so hard she could barely get the words out, and Freddy had looked at her, half pityingly, half satisfied. For a short time, she thinks she's fixed this mess. Put Tabby back in her place. Saved her father from having to read any more of her pathetic messages.

Kept her family together.

It's only later that she realizes her mistake.

She might have made sure Fred didn't come out to meet Tabby, but the mess is far from fixed, and her family far from saved.

"He's watching *Fargo. I* texted you to meet here. So I could tell you how much I hate you, you two-faced, lying slut."

Even through everything piling on top of her right now, the sense of being crushed under the weight of it all, Tabby knows that to some degree, Freddy is right. Fred had abandoned her in her hour of need. She'd never told him she needed him before, never asked for anything. And he couldn't even come and comfort her when her dog was killed.

What a jerk.

She's not even sure if she's referring to Fred, or to herself.

How did Freddy know?

It must have been those texts to the wrong phone, Tabby reasons, and kicks herself. She wonders if Freddy will tell Rebecca. Or Nate. Or Nancy.

She shudders.

She tried really hard not to think about Nancy these whole five months.

She feels the worst about Nancy.

Instinctively, her hand goes to her pocket, to check her phone, but neither phone is in her pocket and she pats herself frantically.

What if Fred was texting?

What if Nate was?

"My phones," she says, panicking.

What if Rebecca found them? Managed to open them? Was holding them when Fred or Nancy messaged?

"I've got it," Leroy says, reaching into his pocket, then frowning. "Wait. It must have fallen out." Leroy realizes he's left his phone behind, too, and shivers. He suddenly feels very alone, on a bridge with Tabby in the middle of the night. He wants to call Nate, or someone. Get backup, get someone who can actually help, instead of just bumbling around like an idiot by himself.

"I don't want Mom to find them," Tabby says, her voicing rising, her hysteria making no sense to Leroy—*would Rebecca finding her phones be any worse than everything else that's just gone wrong?*

"Let's go home," Leroy says softly. "We'll get Gen. We'll go round to your dad's. Until Rebecca has got some help. Or something." Leroy looks uncertain. He's about as certain as Tabby in regards to how to solve this mess. But he does know getting Tabby somewhere warm and safe is at least a first step.

But Tabby just starts to cry again.

"I can't," she says. "There's nothing left for me." She can't explain it to Leroy—she can't admit to falling in love with Fred, or being left hanging by him. She's ashamed that she needs him, that she could be so stupid as to think he really loved her.

Of course he didn't love her.

Nobody loved her.

She can't articulate the depth of despair she feels about Charlie, or Freddy. She can't make any sense of her desperate desire to be loved by her mother, and the murky notion that it must be *her* that is faulty, because mothers love their children, don't they? All of them except her. It's only her whom a mother seems to hate.

In her mind, she knows her mother is wrong. She knows there's something dysfunctional about Rebecca. But in her body, she knows something else.

That she has nothing, is nothing, is not worth loving.

And with sudden ferocity, she lunges to her feet and leaps up onto the thick cobblestone wall of the bridge, the swirling water underneath the only solution her tortured mind can fathom.

41

THURSDAY

Rebecca is marvelling at the bright blue sky.

She can't seem to stop walking. One foot in front of the other. She walks to the bridge where Leroy's car was found. Loses time staring over it.

Pain pulses through her in waves.

What was he doing out here?

She knows the answer to that though.

Trying to comfort her daughter.

What was Tabby doing?

Would a dead dog be enough to inspire her to jump?

Her heart skips a beat.

Rebecca knows it's not just a dead dog, though.

Something has cracked open, between the torrent of thoughts in her head that even a sleeping tablet couldn't slow, and the thought of Genevieve, grieving with her parents, like she might have done.

Should have done.

Somehow, all the pushing down the memories of Moira, all the clamping down the pain, all the pretending it never even happened, seems almost peculiar to Rebecca. And as the memories rush out through that crack, storming out, flooding over her, the surrender seems so much easier than the resistance ever did.

She thinks about Charlie and shivers.

Whatever she's told herself in the past seems suddenly ludicrous. You can yell too much at your kids. You can lose your temper. You can even regret some of the things you say, sometimes.

Regret that surge of power in you, when you see how it crushes someone else.

"*Why does Tabby drive me so crazy*" is no longer the question. Because it doesn't matter. It doesn't matter how crazy Tabby drives her. She still doesn't get to attack her.

Attack.

Rebecca stops abruptly.

Her mind keeps going.

She doesn't get to attack her daughter, emotionally speaking.

And she doesn't get to kill her dog.

Her heart skips another beat. *Did she really do that? Was that really her?*

She looks out at the brilliant spring day, and wonders how she is functioning at all.

Is she not overwhelmed, because she already knows? She's hidden it from herself on the surface for years. But deep down, she knows. She pretended she forgot about the dog. But she didn't forget. She just didn't want to think about it.

Moira's little face drifts in front of her eyes. That look, at the river.

Does everything end at the river?

The uncertainty on Moira's face. Halfway between fear of the river, and a yearning to please her sister. Loving her sister so much she will try to overcome her fear.

That look has haunted Rebecca's dreams for thirty-five years.

She still remembers the coldness. It knocked her breath clean away, like a physical blow. The pull of the current something so unknown, so insistent.

She should have known.

But she didn't.

A lump rises in her throat, a wail caught there, and she swallows and frowns. Quickens her pace and keeps walking. She thinks that if she keeps walking and keeps walking, she will work it out, she will think it all through. Her steps will unravel the tangle she has found herself in.

She has put herself in.

For the first time, she can see that she needs to take ownership of it. This hasn't happened to her. She chooses it. She hides it. Maybe she can change it.

Left, right, left.

Her eyes lose focus.

Left, right, left.

Somehow, her rage toward Tabby is related to Moira, but she can't work it out, it makes her head hurt, it makes everything hurt.

Why am I like this?

Last night's question surfaces again, relentless.

How can I stop?

She shivers.

She knew Leroy was trying to fix it. She knew that's why things were tense between Tabby and him. She knew that, and she took no responsibility herself. And now Leroy was dead, and Tabby was—

God.

Where was Tabby?

Her steps quicken even more.

She's hurrying toward a destination she can't pin down. It's compulsive. This rhythm, this walking. She must keep going.

It's like a drumbeat toward the finale, the climax, a crescendo toward an ending she doesn't want to know, and yet, for the first time, she knows she must. If anything is ever going to be different.

Left, right, left.

She needs to get there, but she doesn't know where "there" is.

She must find Tabby.

Will she ever get a chance to tell her how sorry she is?

What can she say? What does it all mean? How can she explain it?

Will she get a chance to fix it?

Is it even possible?

Here Rebecca stops again. She bends over, hands on her knees. Her eyes aren't clear anymore. And she has the terrible feeling that once she starts crying, she might never, ever stop.

42

DISAPPEARANCE DAY

"No, Tabby!"

Leroy is on his feet immediately, adrenaline surging through him and propelling him up with so much force he goes too far.

He tries to correct himself.

His ankle turns underneath him, and he arcs away from Tabby, his face toward her. Blind panic.

For a moment, it's like he's suspended there, connected to Tabby by his eyes, his mouth open as though he's going to tell her something.

Don't jump.

Live.

I love you.

You'll be okay.

But all she hears is his scream, and a sickening crunch as he hits the rocks below her.

Then a gentle splash.

She lets out a sob, collapsing over the wall, straining to see in the dark.

Later, she'll replay her actions, thinking of all the things she could have done. But what she'll remember is running down the bank, wading into the water, calling Leroy's name.

Feeling more alone than she ever has in her whole entire life.

She'll remember feeling paralyzed, not knowing what to do, crying, cursing her stupidity for leaving her phone behind, for not being able to call for help.

Two phones, and she forgot them both.

There are houses on either side of the river, no more than five hundred meters away, but in her distress, it doesn't even occur to her to knock on a door.

She stumbles around in the river in the dark until she is so cold she thinks she might die, and she wishes, in fact, that she would.

43

THURSDAY

Rebecca walks in the door a minute after Cascy.

She'd started and stopped all the way home.

She needs to tell someone.

Rejection.

The link had suddenly seemed as clear as day. *How did she not see it before?*

When she feels rejected by Tabby.

Nate, too.

When she feels rejected, she loses her mind.

She wants them to love her. She wants to be loved. And when she feels unloved, it's Moira who she sees. Moira who she lost. But she didn't just lose Moira, did she? She lost her parents too. They could never love her after that. How could they?

It's like a movie reel in slow motion.

Click, click, click.

Everything so simple.

She hungers for their love. And when she feels like it is withheld from her, she attacks them so that they're the hurt ones, not her. So she feels powerful, and buries that little secret so far down, it's drowned out by all the other noise.

Unlovable.

The word whispers in her ear, dances and swirls around her, and she had had to stop, sobbing so hard her knees gave out, and she'd collapsed on the sidewalk, great tearing sobs barking from her gaping mouth.

She knew she exerted power to get things.

She just never knew that the things she thought she got—compliance, deference, everything the way she liked it—were not the things she really got.

What she really got was to bury her pain and her shame. She lost her sister, and her parents didn't love her, and the two were tied together, one didn't exist without the other, and she couldn't bear either of them, she couldn't bear anything to feel as bad as that, and she knew how to drown them out, with a roar so loud that no one would ever see them, ever know that they were there.

Most especially herself.

Rebecca stops abruptly.

Casey, Cheryl, Rob, and Nate all stare at her.

Casey speaks first. "We accessed the data on Leroy's phone. You weren't exactly honest with us about why Tabby and Leroy left that night, were you, Rebecca?" Her voice is harder than Nate has heard it, a grinding edge to it that is almost frightening.

He doesn't know what his face belies. He can't truly believe it. For all the hell she's put him through, he just can't believe that Rebecca would kill a dog. As though it was nothing.

He stares at her, as though she could have been any stranger at all, walking in to their old kitchen.

He thought he knew the darkness in her. He thought he had seen her at her worst.

He feels now that he knows nothing.

"No." Rebecca shakes her head. "I lied to you. But that's not the worst thing." Her eyes find Nate's, and there is something new there, something he can't quite place. *Something open, instead of closed? Pain, instead of anger?*

"I was lying to myself, too. Mostly, to myself." She wants to tell Nate, to explain, but four pairs of cold eyes make her falter.

She turns back to Casey.

"I moved Tabby's phone. I tried to get into it, to see if she'd told Leroy anything. I couldn't crack the code. Later, after Gen told us the code, I deleted Tabby's messages to Leroy that night. I know it's all my fault. She was running from me. I didn't want you to see how bad I could be. I didn't want to admit it. Or that I knew Leroy would have been trying to help her. That that's why they left. And I will answer to that. But that's not the most important thing now. The most important thing is finding her. And I think I know where she might be."

"She was going to meet Fred. Gen found her second phone. That fucking creep was sleeping with her." Nate's voice is hard. Even he doesn't know if he's angrier with Fred or with Rebecca.

Rebecca stops, shocked.

But of course she didn't know her daughter. She was too busy blaming everyone else for things that were on her *head.*

"Except Freddy went to meet her instead. They fought. She said she left when Leroy arrived. Said Tabby was crying, and Leroy was trying to comfort her. But she didn't stay, she didn't see what happened."

As this sinks in, Rebecca turns back to Nate. "Let's find her first. Come on." She's so impatient. To find her daughter, check she's okay.

To say sorry.

A million, million sorrys.

There won't be enough days in her life to say all the sorrys that she owes.

She doesn't even know if she can stop thirty of years of reacting one way. Blind rage. But she wants to try. And she knows, intuitively, that now her pain is right there, tangible, engulfing her, her anger might not be so essential anymore. Her anger might not get the upper hand.

"She'll be at your house. You haven't been back since Monday morning. Where else would she go? You're the one she feels safe with. You're the one who feels like home."

For a moment Rebecca holds Nate's eyes. And even as she revolts him, and terrifies him—*the dog, my God, the dog*—he wants to believe in this shift, this openness.

He can't believe that after everything, hope still strains and surges in him.

Is hope a blessing, or a curse?

Nate doesn't think he should trust Rebecca, but the flare of hope exists anyway. But he doesn't have time to process his thoughts, because Rebecca's grabbing her keys, her phone, standing impatiently at the door. Everyone else in the room looks at her in bewilderment, trying to catch up. Then Nate is on his feet.

"We'll stay with Gen," Cheryl says, for the second time that day.

"I'll drive," says Casey, snatching up her keys, kicking herself for not searching Nate's place herself, wondering what exactly her officers did when they went there, *did they even go inside or just knock and leave? And what sort of idiot—*

But Rebecca is already down the steps, into her car, the engine revving. Nate jumps in beside her, and Casey resigns herself to following.

As she backs down the drive, Rebecca pauses long enough to look Nate in the eye again, and holds his gaze.

"I'll fix this," she says. "It might take a long time. But I can see all the things I did, now. I can see how I broke everything. And I promise you. I'll fix it."

Then she throws the car into drive and tears off down the road.

44

ONE WEEK Later

Nancy rests her hand lightly on Freddy's head.

Occasionally she strokes her hair.

Freddy has had it cut short, into a shoulder-length bob.

I don't want to look like her, anymore.

Nancy said nothing. She understands Freddy's anger toward Tabby. She thinks eventually, it might be directed somewhere else. Toward her father. She doesn't interfere, though. She doesn't try to mold her thoughts.

Somehow, Freddy got through her year ten exams, and just shrugged when asked how they went. Nancy doesn't really care about the results, anyway.

She cares that Freddy came to her. Before Nate or Rebecca or Gen or the police.

"She's sleeping with Dad," she'd said. Silently handed her the secret phone.

The text messages were all to one number, except the first two. "Watch your back" and "dirty slut." Freddy had reddened, and admitted she had sent the last three. Nancy thinks to herself that sending messages to Rebecca and Tabby's normal phone kind of went against her plan to keep the affair a secret, but she doesn't say anything. She knows Freddy would not have been thinking clearly.

She asks Freddy what she meant by "watch your back." Freddy says she doesn't know.

"I just wanted them all to feel as bad as I did," she says. "Maybe I was saying Tabby is not trustworthy. Maybe she'll sleep with Leroy too. Or maybe she'll ruin your life, too. I guess I didn't think very hard about it."

The messages to Tabby's secret phone went back to June. Five months of meeting times, sweet nothings, sexting. Nancy didn't read them all—they made her feel sick. She tries to think about what changed in June, or what changed after, but she honestly couldn't say she noticed anything at all.

Are all wives so clueless when their husbands start to fool around?

Maybe Fred had fooled around with teenage girls before. God knows, he was out a lot. For some reason, it's the Saturday afternoons that Nancy keeps getting stuck on. Fred had always claimed he had too much work to take Freddy to her swim meets. Nancy had been taking her all year. Every single Saturday for forty-five weeks. Locally, yes, but also all around bloody Victoria. Admittedly, even before the affair started. But still. To learn that he could premeditatively set aside his "work" to bang Freddy's best friend—a *child*, dammit—filled her with rage.

Anyway, he was gone now.

Nancy didn't ask why Freddy didn't tell her straight away. She didn't want Freddy to feel for even a second that she had done anything wrong. And of course she could guess. She even understands Freddy luring Tabby out to confront her: she imagines Freddy had thought, with the hormone-fuelled and reckless judgement of a sixteen-year-old, that if she could just make Tabby stop it, she could protect Nancy—even Fred—and pretend everything was fine.

Put it all behind them.

For a price.

Now, she looks down at Freddy's face, and her own face is soft, loving. Freddy's eyes are closed, but she's not sleeping. They've been spending evenings together ever since Fred moved out. Sometimes they watch a movie. Sometimes they talk. They always sit close together on the couch.

"Do you want to talk about what happened on the bridge?" Nancy says now, and she feels Freddy stiffen under her fingers. "You don't have to," Nancy adds, her voice gentle. "Just if you want to. Sometimes it helps to talk about the things that hurt us the most."

Freddy doesn't respond. They sit in silence for a while.

"It was me, in Tabby's room that night," Freddy says, eventually. She opens her eyes, but they're unfocused. "Gen said there was a sketch. I wanted to find it. Hide it. Burn it. Something." She lapses into silence, and Nancy just keeps stroking her hair, her fingers light.

"Don't you hate her?" she whispers eventually, and Nancy shakes her head.

"No. She's still a child, Freddy. I know you think you're nearly an adult. But she was in a very vulnerable place. I don't think we can really know what was going on with her mother. But it sounds like it was far worse than any of us realized. Remember you told me a few months ago, that Tabby asked you why you even wanted to be her friend? And you were so confused, it was such a weird thing to ask after you've been friends for so long, and it's so clear that you loved her—"

"Loved," Freddy agrees, emphasizing the past tense, her voice hard.

"Loved," Nancy repeats. "Or maybe love. Maybe feeling so hurt is because it's the people we love the most who can hurt us the most." She pauses, fighting the tears that well in her own eyes, and takes a couple of deep breaths, then goes on, "But it shows how Tabby was feeling about herself, don't you think? She didn't feel secure and loved. And it's hard to make good choices about our relationships from that place. Maybe she was just desperate for someone to love her, and she mistook sex for love with your dad." Something gets stuck in Nancy's throat at those words, "your dad," but she pushes on. "A lot of people do that. A lot of girls, and women, especially."

Nancy is silent for a while. She doesn't want to share her worst thoughts with Freddy about her father. She knows Freddy is going to be confused for long enough about her dad, without having the burden of Nancy's anger, too. But she does feel anger. Anger about the betrayal. But also anger that her husband, who she thought was so good and strong and fair, had preyed on a damaged child for sex. The thought makes her blood boil. It makes her want to kill someone.

Underneath the anger, she knows the pain lies waiting.

However hurt and angry she is, though, what really gets to her is that Fred ignored Tabby when she asked him for help. When her mother had just killed her dog in front of her eyes.

Who was this man she married?

Maybe she didn't want him to have an affair with a barely legal child, but she also didn't want him to be the jerk who was in it only for the sex, and who bailed when anything real was needed of him. The duplicity of her thoughts about this will confuse her for a very long time. *If it was just sex, was it better, or worse?*

"You know," she goes on, thoughtful, "you said Tabby had been so moody lately. I wonder if she found it hard to be with you because she felt guilty about the affair. Sometimes, we just don't have the resources to cope well. I think Tabby does love you. I think she dealt with a shitty situation in the best way she knew how. And it's still a shit way. And I'm not excusing her.

But I feel a bit sad for her, you know? That she didn't have her mom to love and guide her. That in fact her mother's problems might have really pushed her in the wrong direction. And you don't have to ever see her again if you don't want to. But you don't have to decide now. You can take as long as you need. And it would make me really happy if when you ask, 'How could she do that to me?' if you really think deeply about the answer. Because I don't believe she's a mean girl who was trying to hurt you. I think she was coping imperfectly with some pretty sad things in her own life. And they may mean that she can never be the friend to you that you want her to be, and that's okay. And it's totally okay to be angry and sad. But whatever Tabby did, it's not about you, okay, Freddy? It's not a reflection on you, and your value as a friend. It's a reflection on her and how she feels about herself. And you get to decide what happens now. Sometimes, people just don't stay in our lives forever, and that's okay too."

In private, Nancy won't be so reasonable. She'll rage and scream and hate Tabby, too, for a time. She'll call her own friends and cry and rant, over and over. But for Freddy, she can put herself aside.

For Freddy, she can be exactly who Freddy needs her to be to get through this.

She knows that nothing has ever mattered so much.

And she knows they wouldn't be having this conversation now if Rebecca had been able to do that for her own daughter. So she puts her pain aside in front of Freddy, and strokes her daughter's hair with all the love and calmness that she can muster.

ACROSS TOWN, another parent sits on another couch with another girl.

"Thank you for telling me." Nate has one arm around Genevieve. He's holding Tabby's hand with his other arm.

Both girls are circumspect. The house feels empty and daunting.

Rebecca has gone to stay in a hotel for a couple of weeks, while she finds a therapist to support her to manage the days and weeks and months ahead. She agreed that it was important for the girls to be in their own home, and that Nate should stay with them there until he found a bigger place. But they'll see Rebecca today for Leroy's funeral.

The revelations about Moira had crashed into their lives with so much force Nate didn't know how any of them managed to stand up from the table. After they got Tabby home, there was so much pain to unpack it felt like they sat at that table for months, talking.

It was only a day, of course.

Later, when Tabby was asleep, exhausted and spent, not believing her father's assurances she wasn't to blame, not believing Rebecca's assurances she was going to change, Rebecca had shouted and screamed at her parents: "You did blame me! You blamed me with every look and every action for the next six years!" And they had sobbed and sobbed and sobbed.

"No," Cheryl had said, shaking her head emphatically. "Whatever you felt, that was us blaming ourselves. It was the thing that made us see how badly we were treating you, how much we were taking out on you that wasn't your fault. Everyone told us we'd never survive. Moira's death, right after the affair. But somehow we kept going, together. And we tried. You refused to talk about it. You withdrew into yourself. We could never reach you."

"You never tried!" Rebecca was sobbing too, and it was utter chaos in the kitchen. Like thirty years of grief had washed in through the windows and they were all drowning in pain, thrashing about, fighting for life. Nate had cried too: for Moira, for Cheryl, for Rob, for Tabby, and even for Rebecca.

"We did try," Cheryl said. "But we gave up too soon. And we think about it and regret it every single day of our lives."

To himself, Nate thinks that there's a gaping chasm between realizing how badly you failed, and doing everything you need to do to fix it. Cheryl and Rob have not even come close. *What did trying even look like? How much does wanting to fix it count for, in the end, if you don't? If you just leave it to get passed on, and on, and on?*

Then he looks at Rebecca, and at himself, and his thoughts quiet.

Wasn't he just the same as them?

Like Nancy, Nate doesn't need to ask Gen why she didn't come to him about Tabby and Fred. *How can you make good decisions when you're fourteen years old? How can you make good decisions about such complex things when you don't trust your parents to protect you?* Every time he thinks about it his heart plummets to his feet. The thought of Gen alone, trying to solve this problem, is almost unbearable.

Nevertheless, she had tried to explain: "I just wanted it to stop. I thought Freddy would make Tabby see, would make it stop. I knew it would be bad for Tabby, that Fred was just using her. And getting rid of Fred would be bad for a while, but better once she got over him. I just wanted her to be okay." Here Gen breaks down in tears, and Nate does, too.

"It's not your job, sweetheart. It's my job. And I was failing at it, and I'm sorry you thought you had to take over."

"No one ever talks about it. You knew. And Mom knew. And Leroy knew. And no one ever just said it. Everyone just tiptoed around pretending we were fine and normal. Like every family worked like this."

"Is that why things were tense between Leroy and Tabby?" Nate can't quite grasp why Tabby would blame Leroy, rather than Rebecca. He looks to Tabby for an answer, but her eyes are vacant. He's not even sure she heard.

"Leroy was safe to be angry with, I suppose. He didn't help, but he tried. Maybe it was easier to be angry with him for failing, than with Mom for being how she is in the first place."

Nate stares at Genevieve.

He thinks the shame and the pain might actually kill him, it feels so bad.

All the time he wasted accusing Leroy, imagining awful and creepy things, instead of actually listening to his children. And God, Tabby asked to move in with him. And even after all that bitching about Leroy, he didn't put his money where his mouth was. If he was really concerned, wouldn't he have said yes, made it work? Did he just want to complain without taking any responsibility? Even if his motives were dodgy, he could have gotten Tabby somewhere safe. He could have started to help her.

He shoves his fists into his eyes. He doesn't mind Genevieve seeing him cry, but howling like he feels compelled to do seems too raw, too unfair, too much to burden her with.

At the same time, he wants to just stare at her in wonder.

"You knew what she could drive a person to," Gen says now. She doesn't look at Nate. She has that defiant jut to her chin again, and he wonders how many times he will need to apologize, and show he's fixing it, before she will trust him again. He doesn't wonder in frustration. He will show her over and over again for as long as it takes.

"That message you sent. To that woman. We knew why you sent it. You didn't know. And Mom didn't know. But we did."

Nate starts. He remembers that fight like it was yesterday. No matter how hard he's tried to shove it out of mind.

Rebecca had pounced on it, used it to tell him that he was just like her—with a bad temper. Abusing people. But they weren't the same. They were connected together, sure. That he was so worn down by it, so pummelled by it, like a cornered cat, he just attacked the next person who came near him, who he felt threatened by.

Someone safer to attack than his wife.

"I did know," he says softly. "I just didn't think that it impacted you. I thought it was just about me. I was wrong. I didn't think hard enough. I took the easy route."

He starts to cry again. *How is it that his teenage daughters can see things so much more clearly than he can himself?*

Tabby isn't saying anything.

She's holding his hand though. Holding it tight. And that's a start. It's not enough. He has to do better. But this week, this month, this year, even—his daughter still wants to hold his hand, and the relief and gratitude he feels is monumental.

When they opened Nate's front door, Rebecca running up the front path, trying to take his keys from him, her urgency palpable, Tabby had said nothing.

She looked as though she hadn't eaten since she left on Sunday night. Always tiny, her hips now jutted out above the waist of her jeans in a way that seemed somehow cruel to Nate. Screaming at him just how badly he had let this child down. She had circles under her eyes so dark she was almost unrecognizable. And her eyes themselves were so vacant, uncomprehending almost.

Nate could barely tolerate that she had been suffering alone. He wanted to howl, to grasp her so tightly nothing could ever hurt her ever again, to fall at her feet.

Forgive me, forgive, me, forgive me.

But he held himself together, pulling her into his arms, kissing her temple. "You're okay, you're okay," he said, over and over, like if he said it enough they would all believe it was true.

But it was Rebecca whose eyes she finally found, coming slowly back to them, gaunt, haunted. Like she'd aged a thousand years.

Casey hung back, in the doorway, watching them quietly, on edge.

Rebecca stepped forward, sure of herself, and reached for Tabby's hand. Tabby let her take it, but it was limp, lifeless. Her eyes lost focus again, drifting away.

"I'm so sorry, Tab," Rebecca had whispered, her eyes fixed on Tabby's vacant ones, and Nate had watched for some menace, some harshness, ready to spring in to action, to wrestle Tabby away from her, to protect her, God help him, for the rest of his life, but Rebecca's hands were soft over Tabby's. She didn't look like the Rebecca he knew. She looked broken and gentle and like she didn't know what to do.

Tabby had turned from her though, and buried her face in Nate's shoulder. "I killed him. It's my fault. It's my fault." She was barely audible, her shoulders heaving. Her tiny frame seemed too small, too young, to have to carry such a burden for a single minute, let alone for four days, alone in his house.

Or the rest of her life.

"It's not your fault," Rebecca had said, her voice firm. "It's my fault. It's my fault you ran away, it's my fault Leroy followed you." She doesn't know what to do, or how to fix it, but she knows that much. "I'm sorry, Tabby. I'm going to—" Here she faltered though. *What is she going to do? Be better? How can she know such a thing? She doesn't want to lie to Tabby.* She had taken a jagged breath. "I don't know how to fix it. But I'm going to try."

Slowly, slowly Tabby emerged from Nate's chest. Her voice was vacant, like she was far, far away. "You'll just buy me another dress, though, right, Mom?" She dragged her eyes up to Rebecca's. Nate held his breath. Something in Tabby's eyes caught in his throat, spiky and lumpy and heart-wrenching. Like she'd dragged up some bravado, some spite, but underneath, she was longing for Rebecca's words to be true. For her to be sorry, and to fix it.

For Rebecca to be the mother she always wished she would be.

Even after all the times she'd been let down, there was still a tiny seedling of hope growing there, and Tabby was working to crush it by provoking her mother, by making the inevitable happen, by fast tracking it so it was over, and she could know.

Nate thought his heart couldn't break any more, but it does.

But then, Rebecca leaned in closer to Tabby, never looking away, her face soft.

"No more dresses," she whispered, and Nate started to cry.

Now, Nate holds his girls to him.

He can see how far Tabby is from forgiving herself. He catches her staring at a photo of Rebecca and Leroy on their wedding day, and worries the grief and guilt will crush her.

Once, he found her with an unsent text message open to Nancy. She hastily shut the phone when he walked past.

He's organized for her to see a therapist. Gen too.

Cheryl and Rob have offered to come back down when Rebecca returns, to support them for as long as they need, with whatever they need.

They have a long way to go. But Nate has never been so proud of them, and he tells them so.

Tabby looks disbelieving. "Leroy's dead because of me. Nancy's marriage is over. Freddy hates me." Her voice is leaden.

"And I betrayed my sister," Gen says dully. "Tabby and Leroy would never have gone to that bridge if I hadn't told Freddy." She starts quietly to cry.

"But you're both here. You're both talking about it. You're showing up, which is more than your mother and I have done. We could learn a thing or two from you both. You've done amazing things with a shit hand. It wasn't your job to solve this.

It was our job. So if anyone is at fault, it's your mother and me. Not you, do you understand? And I know that won't mean you stop feeling bad. And we will support you through that. For as long as it takes. But everything you did, you shouldn't have had to think about, or decide about. You should have been able to come to us. And you couldn't, and that's on us. Not you."

Nate believes this so much he fears that he might drown in it, but he knows it will take more than one speech to shift his daughters' thinking.

He thinks about Rebecca, and how she had tried to outpace her pain, tried to squash it down and refuse it like her life depended on it, and where it had led them all. He knows Tabby and Gen can't go around it. They have to sit in it, and it fills him with terror. That he can't protect them. That he can't fix it for them. That he can't—and shouldn't—make it go away.

He can sit with them through it, though.

"Are you ready?" he says now, and both girls nod numbly.

"Your mom will meet us there. You choose if you want to talk to her. If you don't want to, she understands. Whenever you're ready, she'll be there, okay? If you want to go to her, go. If you want me to help you, I can do that. Whatever you need, we'll work it out, okay?"

Neither girl meets his eyes, and Nate wonders if the bricks will ever get off his chest, if this pain will ever go away. But he takes both their hands and leads them out to the car.

45

DETECTIVE CASEY STANDS at the back of the room.

The service was simple. Leroy's father delivered the eulogy, dry-eyed. There was something stoic about him, but Casey could feel the sadness radiating from the podium.

He spoke about Leroy's love for his family, and made the audience laugh with an anecdote about how he and Rebecca had met. Rebecca was his first and only wife, and Leroy's family seemed to love her.

Rebecca spoke, too. She was composed, and Casey watched with interest. Her words were awash with contained grief and regrets. Though Casey doubted anyone knew the details of what happened that night—the official story was that Tabby had fought with Rebecca and run away, and Leroy had gone to find her, and found her on the bridge wall—Rebecca's words hinted at all the things she wished she'd done differently.

Casey's eyes wander around the room, and come to rest on Tabby. She's dressed in black pants that hang limply off her hips, and a dark blue shirt. She leans on Nate, and somehow manages to look dishevelled or crumpled, despite her well-pressed, well-cut clothes. Nate has one arm around her. Her shoulders judder slightly, and Casey thinks she is crying, quietly, discreetly.

At the station, Tabby had recounted what had happened in fits and starts.

Despite Nate's rage—he had sat with her through her statement—her affair had started with Fred just weeks after she had turned sixteen, and legally, there was nothing they could do. She'd recounted how it started in a dull voice, her face lifeless.

When she spoke about running from the house, asking Fred to help her, then leaping onto the bridge in despair, Nate couldn't stop the strangled noise in his throat. There was so much to be enraged about he had no words.

Tabby had remained dry-eyed.

"Are you still thinking about ending your life?" Casey had asked, gentle, glancing at Nate. Suspecting he wouldn't know how to broach this topic, or what to do next if Tabby said yes.

She'd dragged her eyes back to Casey, and shrugged. "My life doesn't look so great right now, does it?" She held Casey's eyes for a moment, then dipped her face back down and mumbled, "But no. I don't even want to get out of bed, let alone do anything that requires more effort."

Casey had sent Nate off with a number to call to link Tabby in with a clinician, not just to manage her risk, but to support her through the long months ahead. She hopes that he has called it.

Now, mourners file out of the funeral home into the bright spring day. Casey hangs back, until the room is nearly empty. Outside, Rebecca stands next to Leroy's parents, shaking hands and accepting condolences. Casey nods at her as she goes past.

In interview, she had been surprisingly forthcoming. She'd even asked if Casey knew where she could get help with her anger, and Casey had been stumped. Usually she'd refer to a Men's Behavior Change program, but she'd never even heard of one for women. At the same time, after hearing about what happened to Leroy, to Moira, and the pain and recriminations in that family, she thought perhaps Rebecca should start there. She gave her the number of a therapist she trusted. And gently suggested that though addressing her anger was important, that perhaps she needed to start with her grief.

"It's going to be a long road," she'd said, watching Rebecca. Wondering if she meant it, if she really wanted to change. "Change is hard. And it sounds like you have a lot of pain to work through. A lot of fractured relationships to repair. And maybe, making a plan, with a concrete outcome, is more of the same. Maybe you need to sit with how much it all hurts for a while." To her surprise, Rebecca had allowed the tears that welled in her eyes, and nodded.

Casey does think that, if anyone is going to do what she sets her mind to, it's probably Rebecca.

She thinks about Charlie, and her heart hardens. But then she thinks about Moira, and it softens again.

They don't press charges about the dog. Neither Tabby nor Nate want anything further to happen about it, and Casey thinks this family has enough pain to contend with. She thinks that if they're going to get out of this alive, they're going to need support, not punishment.

As she walks back to her car, she sees Nate, one arm around each of his daughters.

"I've moved back in to Rebecca's house, while we try to get through this," he'd told her earlier that week, hastily adding, "Not in a romantic way. Just in a family way. To make things a bit more stable for the girls. To support them, and Rebecca, too." His eyes had drifted away, over her head, unfocused, and she thought that maybe he would support them all, maybe they would all be okay. With time, and external support, too.

Where do you even start to recover from something like this?

Now, she meets his eyes as she passes. She doesn't quite

smile. She hopes her body language conveys her acknowledgement that he's there. He's trying. She hopes he will do better.

She's rooting for him, even.

Then she steps off the curb and gets in to her car.

EPILOGUE

Six Months Later

When Rebecca gets home from work, Nate hands her a gin.

She smiles at him, and asks about his day.

"Same, same," he murmurs, following her out to the veranda, where they sit in silence for a while.

In truth, it had been a hard day. Tabby has bad days, sometimes. And somehow her bad days overflow onto Genevieve, and they're all having a bad day. But that's okay.

Now, Tabby comes out the front door, and startles when she sees her parents sitting there. She bristles, her eyes frosty. "I'm going to work," she says. She glances at Rebecca, a long sideways glance. There's something slightly spiteful about it. She knows she doesn't need to say any more. She'd explained it all clearly enough when she first starting volunteering at the women's refuge. How she wanted to help other people like her.

At the time, she'd been teary and idealistic. Fresh off her new understanding of her mother, she launched herself into this new endeavor, wanting to support all the hurt people in the world. Nate and Rebecca had been tentatively supportive. They'd worried, parental, over coffee, whether she needed to be directing that inward, and helping herself, rather than outward, and supporting others. But in the end they'd agreed that a sense of purpose seemed galvanizing for their daughter. She had something to believe in, something that was getting her out of bed.

Also, the refuge had her doing administrative things off-site at the organization's office, not actively supporting distressed women at the refuge location. So they were supportive and attentive. They asked questions and listened to difficult answers.

Now, Rebecca can see the accusation in Tabby's eyes.

I'm going to work to help all the women crushed by people like you, her eyes say, daring Rebecca to revert to type. Still just waiting for it. Bracing for it.

She'd been waiting for six months, and it hadn't happened yet.

Rebecca isn't complacent, though. She still *feels* the familiar rage. She still grapples with it. She just has better resources to make a different choice when it rears its ugly head.

She also has Nate still living with them, offering support and, she supposes, a judgmental eye. She thinks about him moving back out and feels a flash of panic. Well, he can't for now. Her parents are staying at his house. They've been amazing, even Rebecca has to admit that. Taking the girls to therapy, sometimes twice a week. Coming by to cook dinner on days where Rebecca feels overwhelmed, or unable to cope. Sometimes just sitting with her when she has all the feelings, but none of the words. Last week, they brought an old shoe box full of photos. They didn't open it. They popped it in the cupboard above the fridge, and told her it was there. "For if and when you're ready," Cheryl had said. Rebecca could see how hard she was working not to cry.

She hadn't looked in the shoebox yet. She wants to. But she's not ready yet.

"What time will you finish?" she asks her daughter. "Nate or I can pick you up, if it's going to be late." Usually Tabby does a couple of hours after school during business hours. Tonight is the first time she's been asked to help out after hours. The thought makes Rebecca anxious. There will be less staff around. Whatever Tabby tells her about the nature of her role, she can't help worry that perhaps Tabby will need to call the refuge, might be exposed to more distress. Or even vengeful exes, who can't find out the location of the refuge, and turn up to the office instead.

She still has trouble equating these men's behaviors to her own. She has to remind herself. *I did that. I did that, too.*

She still has to make conscious space for Tabby to be working through her own pain and her own healing in this way. With something so riling, so close to her own pain, her own healing. *Of all the things to choose, Tabby chose one that forces her to think about her own behavior, every day.*

Rebecca supposes there's something unconsciously just right about that.

"I'm okay on my bike," Tabby says, and hesitates, looking from Nate to Rebecca and back again. Rebecca finds she is having trouble keeping her breath steady. She knows what Tabby is thinking: *can I kiss Dad goodbye, and not Mom?* She knows that when Tabby thinks she's alone with Nate, she always kisses him goodbye.

When Nate is with Rebecca, she kisses neither of them.

"Well, just call if it gets later than you thought, or if you change your mind. You know you can call Nan, too, if you prefer." Calling Cheryl "Nan" feels so weird to Rebecca, but that's what both Cheryl and the girls seem to prefer, so Rebecca had asked if she should refer to her that way too. Cheryl, as usual, looked as though she might cry.

Unspoken in those words, is Rebecca conveying: *I know you might be more comfortable with anyone but me. I accept that. I will keep working on it. Forever.* At first she thought she had to say them out loud, over and over. But her therapist told her she just had to show Tabby that that was the case.

She puts more thought into how to do that than in any other thing she has ever done.

Now, Tabby dithers on the deck. Then she comes to a decision. She steps closer to them, and leans down to kiss Nate on the cheek. "Bye, Dad," she says.

Then without missing a beat, she leans over to Rebecca, too. "Bye, Mom," she says, her eyes flicking to Rebecca's, then she plants a kiss firmly on Rebecca's cheek, then turns on her heel and skips lightly down the stairs, her ponytail swinging.

She doesn't look back, and Nate and Rebecca watch her wheel her bike from the shed in amicable silence.

Then she swings one leg over and pedals away.

ALSO BY

Praise for The Good Daughter

"Mind-opening...Fascinating, frightening, very deep. Learned a great deal about human nature, suffering, and redemption... These characters are so real to me. An unforgettable, compassionate account. Many thanks to this author for tackling extremely difficult family dynamics, and for doing it so well!" ★★★★★ *Apple books review*

"What a thrilling story, with so much thought going in to every sentence. A very sensitive subject matter, but superbly written. It really grips you from the very first page. I highly recommend this book, you won't be able to put it down." ★★★★ *Amazon review*

"...fast moving and intriguing. A surprise ending. I recommend reading." ★★★★ *Amazon review*

"Wow! This book was not what I expected. It was extremely fast paced and dealt with many provocative subjects. Natalie, the main character, is very strong and I was pulled into her struggle instantly. This is a very thought-provoking, compelling, and complex thriller." ★★★★ *Amazon review*

"Liane Moriarty, but grittier." - *Catherine Deveny, Writer, Comedian, Author and Speaker*

"This is a story that will stay with me for a long time." ★★★★ *Amazon review*

"I am in awe of this writer and this story. It was so gritty and emotional and so compelling. I couldn't put it down. The emotions that ran thru and the intrigue kept you guessing...I don't say this often, this is a story not to be missed." ★★★★★ *Amazon review*

"This complex story took me by surprise. It is like nothing I have ever read. The characters are well written and developed. They are realistic and captivating. All of them had secrets...this is a book not to be overlooked. It is a must read." ★★★★★ *Amazon review*

"This story is brilliantly written and really grips you, keeping you guessing until the very end. I can usually tell how it will end or whodunnit but this time no matter how convinced I was about who it was, I was wrong and I love that!" ★★★★★ *Goodreads review*

"It's thrilling, a little scary, and intriguing...Hint: Your first, second, and third guesses are all wrong."★★★★★ *Amazon review*

"This book was impossible to put down. Its a total page turner – intelligent, well-written and thoughtful content, intriguing story and topical themes. Highly recommend." ★★★★★ *Amazon review*

THE GOOD DAUGHTER

A VIOLENT MURDER.

A family secret.

And a boyfriend who's not who he says he is...

Sydney, Australia. Lawyer and companion Natalie Coommaraswamy struggles to be the good daughter her parents demand. A second-generation Sri Lankan, she's never penetrated her family's resolute silence surrounding their flight from Sri Lanka, and has been left with unanswered questions about where she belongs and who she can trust.

Then her best friend is found murdered. Fuelled by disinterest from the police, Natalie begins her own hunt for the murderer. But when clues point to her new lover, her carefully regulated world starts to unravel. And the truth will threaten more than her sanity...

Praise for The Lost Boy

"This story was intense and sorrowful. I connected with Olivia and Nick, and even after finishing the story, my soul is heavy, and my mind swirls. This author is thought-provoking, and her writing is deep and powerful." ★★★★★ *Amazon review*

"Really enjoying S.A McEwen's books. They are real, gritty and look at issues in Australian society that are very current. Great depth of characters that show multifaceted ranges of depth and emotions." ★★★★★ *Amazon review*

"A well-written page-turner that kept me guessing until the end. I had a hard time putting it down! The characters are intriguing and well-drawn, and the story has many twists and turns that I didn't see coming." ★★★★ *Amazon review*

"Smart, fast-moving, twisty and dark...perfect for fans of *The Last Thing He Told Me* and *Little Fires Everywhere*." ★★★★★ *Amazon review*

"Beautifully written, tightly plotted page-turner." ★★★★★ *Amazon review*

THE LOST BOY

THE HAPPIEST-LOOKING *families sometimes hide the darkest secrets...*

In a quiet Melbourne suburb, a young boy vanishes from his front yard without a trace.

Thrust into the limelight, his parents start to unravel. The more time that elapses with no leads, the more public opinion starts to swing from sympathy to suspicion, and the image of the perfect family starts to crack under the increasing scrutiny of the media and the police.

The boy's mother, Olivia, knows better than anyone that even the happiest-looking families harbor secrets.

And the nightmare is closer than she thinks...

Sister in Trouble - coming June 2022

ADELE FRENCH LOST HER SISTER, Celia, fifteen years ago, and she's never stopped looking for answers or someone to blame.

Now, human remains have been found near the home Celia once shared with her husband, Albert.

Adele thinks she can finally put her sister to rest. Not to mention the ugly lies that Albert fabricated about Celia after she disappeared. She's determined to uncover the truth about the night Celia vanished, and see justice served at last.

But Adele told some lies, too, back then.

And if you dig for secrets in dark places, you can't always control what comes to light...

VISIT WWW.SAMCEWEN.COM TO preorder on your preferred store.

AUTHOR'S NOTE

I read a lot of brilliant non-fiction in my professional life. One of the stand out books this year was Jess Hill's *See What You Made Me Do*. I found it fascinating, particularly in regards to the researchers who posit that all violence begins with shame.

I want to acknowledge that the overwhelming majority of people who employ coercive control and use violence against their partners are men. However, I had a personal experience that made me curious about what it looked like in women, and the phrase 'humiliated fury' really rang true to me. It's heavy going, but I highly recommend the book if you are interested in the topic.

I'd also like to acknowledge that I gave Nate a lot more depth, remorsefulness and understanding than the people who send violent messages to women online might warrant (I'm thinking of the work done by feminist Clementine Ford and the astounding abuse she cops on a regular basis). I'm not sure that a man like Nate would really send a message like that, or be so readily reformed. That type of behaviour is usually part of a broader pattern of misogynistic behaviour.

ACKNOWLEDGMENTS

To Stephanie—well quite frankly, you get an F for alpha reading this time around, but still a million thank you for talking to me about your work in Men's Behaviour Change, as well as All the Big Things, All the Time.

Sarah M, Amy Vox Libris, and Kirsten Moore—thank you once again. Your insights and thoughts have been invaluable. I feel so lucky to have you read early drafts and give such wonderful feedback.

To Erica Russikoff from Erica Edits—thank you once again for being generally brilliant. But also for being so encouraging and so interested in my stories and just so lovely. It really means more than you know :)

To @rghdrftstudio for another beautiful cover—thank you.

And to all of you reading this book—thank you. I really appreciate it, and I hope that you enjoyed it. x

ABOUT THE AUTHOR

S.A. McEwen writes nuanced and gritty psychological/domestic thrillers exploring relationships, especially within families... with a particular interest in how the dark gets in, and the complex things that drive us toward or keep us out of connection with each other

She is a qualified social worker and educator in youth mental health, and lives in Melbourne with two gorgeous boys and a puppy.

If you've enjoyed her writing, please get in touch and say hello! The links are listed below.

Get notified when I **release a new book** via my newsletter here: www.samcewen.com.

- facebook.com/authorsamcewen
- amazon.com/author/samcewen
- bookbub.com/authors/s-a-mcewen
- goodreads.com/samcewen
- instagram.com/samcewenwrites